Praise for Alan Judd

Mail on Sunday

'Belongs to the classic tradition of spy writing'
Guardian

'Judd infuses his writing with insider knowledge'
New Statesman

'Wonderful. One of the best spy novels ever'
Peter Hennessy on *Legacy*

'Entertaining and compulsively readable'
Melvyn Bragg on *A Breed of Heroes*

'Fascinating . . . if one of the hallmarks
of a good novel is that the characters do not
remain static but are subtly transformed by
events, then this is a very good novel indeed'
Sunday Telegraph

'Judd is a masterful storyteller, with
an intricate knowledge of his subject and
a sure command of suspense'
Daily Telegraph

'Rivetingly accurate'
Observer

SHAKESPEARE'S SWORD

Also by Alan Judd

Fiction
A Breed of Heroes
Short of Glory
The Noonday Devil
Tango
The Devil's Own Work
Legacy
The Kaiser's Last Kiss
Dancing with Eva
Uncommon Enemy
Inside Enemy
Slipstream
Deep Blue

Non-Fiction
Ford Madox Ford (biography)
*The Quest for C: Mansfield Cumming and
the Founding of the Secret Service* (biography)
First World War Poets (with David Crane)

ALAN JUDD

From the acclaimed author of *Deep Blue*

SHAKESPEARE'S SWORD

SIMON &
SCHUSTER

London · New York · Sydney · Toronto · New Delhi

A CBS COMPANY

First published in Great Britain by Simon & Schuster UK Ltd, 2018
A CBS COMPANY

1 3 5 7 9 10 8 6 4 2

Simon & Schuster UK Ltd
1st Floor
222 Gray's Inn Road
London WC1X 8HB

Simon & Schuster Australia, Sydney
Simon & Schuster India, New Delhi

www.simonandschuster.co.uk
www.simonandschuster.com.au
www.simonandschuster.co.in

A CIP catalogue record for this book
is available from the British Library

Paperback ISBN: 978-1-4711-7819-1
eBook ISBN: 978-1-4711-6714-0

Typeset in Sabon by M Rules
Printed and bound by CPI Group (UK) Ltd, Croydon, CR0 4YY

FOREWORD

by James Naughtie

Two people enter an antique shop. They look at some porcelain, then an Edwardian roll-top desk. Nothing much happens, except that between them and the dealer in the shop there's a surge of electricity.

Mysterious, unsourced, and dangerous.

By the time they leave after a few minutes, their business uncompleted, a story has started to weave itself around them that's already prickling with fear.

Then, another moment.

A throwaway glance, and an idea. From somewhere, the memory of six words in Shakespeare's will. Could that dusty, battered length of steel, being used as a poker, conceal a glittering history of its own?

The elements of this story combine quickly and with the fire of a sudden chemical reaction. In other words, Alan Judd demonstrates again that he understands the elusive secret of narrative. Eyes meet, there's a touch on the arm, a stab of insight, and a tale begins to unfold.

'You mean you're an opportunist?' the woman says to the dealer, and cuts him to the quick. However, it unravels, with many a twist, we know that it will bring destruction.

The satisfaction of a short novel that can be consumed easily in one or two sittings is that it celebrates that intensity. Nothing is wasted, not a glance nor a shudder of self-reflection.

'I've long suspected there's something missing in me,' says Simon Gold, the dealer. And we think we begin to understand him. Nothing will surprise us, and we should prepare.

Judd likes to talk about his life – 'soldier and diplomat' – with elliptical grace, but he is certainly an observer by trade. So much of his fiction thrives on the mysterious complications that arise from the simplest of incidents or remarks, or an odd collision of events. Whether in the Kaiser's last days after the First World War, or in an English country house where memories are stirred of Hitler and Eva Braun together, or in his Charles Thoroughgood spy stories, everything depends on the telling detail that is easy to miss but, when seen, can explain everything.

That giveaway smile or a childlike attempt at deception; the unnecessary word that brings trouble in its wake, the silence that shouldn't be there and raises a troubling question. It's an atmosphere that brings to mind above all the stories of Patricia Highsmith.

Like some of her masterly books – think of Ripley, the smiling psychopath – *Shakespeare's Sword* succeeds in bringing together a suffocating feeling of inevitability with the thrill of surprise. When that happens, you have a story. The journey of Simon Gold is shaped by chance and fate, and leaves every reader wondering, from start to finish, what is true and what is not. We have to know, even if no one wants to tell us.

A country antique dealer, in a sleepy world but prey to emotions that are hidden to others, is bound on his own wheel of fire.

'No one in his right mind should ever really want to know what others think of him and the truer it is the more it rankles, even when said in jest or well meant.' Perhaps especially when it is well-meant.

To one of the people whom he hopes understands him, he says, 'Our end is where nothing matters, but until we get there I suppose you would say that it does.' How can any reader not want to join that journey?

This is a quick adventure, fearful and comic, from a writer with an ear for the subtleties of the most apparently-innocent conversation, in which nothing is as it first seems. And it's a reminder that one chance encounter and a few interlocking glances can be the gateway to a dark labyrinth. *Shakespeare's Sword* is a little gem of storytelling.

To David Crane
and Honor Clerk

Chapter One

I was not, I assured her, an obsessive. Nothing like it. I have come across many obsessives during decades in the antiques trade and know what to look for: unobtrusiveness, immunity to distraction, a furtive wariness of competition. And, of course, knowledge so detailed that once they open the sluice gates you are swept away by the torrent. But she never believed me, not really, and you could argue that events proved her right.

I have a seventeenth-century lantern clock that was here in the shop when I bought the lease. It has never worked (it is 'awaiting restoration' – which means I won't spend money on it until there is a prospective buyer) and has gradually retreated from the front window, to the display case beneath the counter, to one of the wall display cases and finally to the upper back shelf where it has stood, ignored or forgotten, through generations of other stock.

Then one day a man came in and asked to see it. He was middle-aged, bald and shabbily dressed. His face hadn't felt a razor for some time and he wore dirty jeans with worn-out trainers and no socks. He wanted to see the clock and showed no more interest in anything else in the shop than in his own appearance. His voice was confident and educated. I had to get the stepladder to bring the clock down, telling him that, as ticketed by the previous owner, it was probably made in the 1690s by Richard Savage of Much Wenlock. He took it from me without a word, turned it to the light and within thirty seconds had told me that it was not a Savage but probably the work of an apprentice or imitator. The top and bottom plates were iron rather than the more expensive brass Savage used. He was known to have made only two lantern clocks using iron in this way, of which this man owned one. My clock, he told me after further study, was an interesting but crude effort, probably the work of another rural clockmaker at the beginning of a career that never developed. There was an inappropriate twentieth-century replacement hammer spring which, he was sure, I would wish to replace before selling. The clock was not worthless – far from it – but it was of no interest to him. I learned later that he was a very wealthy former pop singer who lived about twenty miles away and had learned to make clocks himself.

That was the man I had in mind when I assured her

I was nothing like an obsessive. I am more a magpie, a snapper-up of unconsidered trifles, knowing a little about a lot but not very much about anything. That is how I learned to survive in business. Deep knowledge would never have paid the lease but a quick eye and a facility for sensing what people wanted, nimbleness rather than real expertise, is why I am still here and the two other serious dealers in this town have closed.

What provoked her accusation was that I had thrice corrected her on the attribution of some porcelain pieces in one of the display cases. They were Sèvres, not Meissen, I told her. Probably early Sèvres. Her manner was playful when she accused me of being an obsessive but it was still an unusually provocative – even flirtatious – remark to make to someone you'd first met about a minute and a half before. I think I must have overdone my response – too earnest, perhaps, or maybe I stood too close – because she stepped back.

'You mean you're an opportunist?' she said. Although she said it with a smile there was a fractional change in the skin tone on her cheeks, a slight tightening which deepened the crow's feet around her eyes. She had – has – the most beautiful eyes, a deep impenetrable blue, almost misty in a way that makes you suspect she's short-sighted, though she isn't. She may have feared I was going to go on about myself, obsessively.

ALAN JUDD

I didn't like being labelled an opportunist, either. No one in his right mind should ever really want to know what others think of him and the truer it is the more it rankles, even when said in jest or well meant. Early in our marriage my former wife told me that her mother had tried to warn her off me, saying I was a 'drifter'. I wasn't quite sure what she meant but it was a dart that struck home, true in a way I could sense but not see. I was indignant at the time, and still am. It was my wife who drifted.

I smiled at my potential customer. 'Just a survivor. So far.'

'What do you think of this, darling?' At the sound of her husband's voice her expression changed, the playfulness hardening into a particular set of the mouth which I was to come to know well.

'Coming, darling.' They dear'd and darling'd each other frequently, as I would also come to know well.

She joined him in the other half of the shop, the brown-furniture half, screened by two nineteenth-century Welsh oak dressers, identical twins made for a manor in Shropshire. Beautiful pieces which I'd been pleased to get because it's so rare to find twins but, like most old brown furniture these days, increasingly difficult to move on. Unfashionable and too big for most modern houses, especially as a pair, they suffered the blight that has now extended even to Georgian furniture, for years a reliable seller.

I'd seen her husband when they entered, a stout man of later middle-age who looked older than her, with heavy-framed glasses, blue blazer, white open-necked shirt, pressed khaki trousers, polished brown shoes. While she lingered by the small stuff he disappeared behind those two dressers, which I used as a false wall to compartmentalise the shop and make it seem bigger. I had the impression he had spotted something through the window.

I returned to my desk while they whispered out of sight, mainly a deep rumble from him punctuated by her monosyllabic interjections. After a couple of minutes she reappeared from behind the dressers. 'Could you please ...?'

I joined them. He was standing before an Edwardian mahogany roll-top desk, an unusually nice piece, unrestored and with its original key. 'What can you tell me about this?' he said.

He played with it while we discussed it, opening and shutting everything that moved. It was clear that he didn't know what he was looking at but equally clear that he felt he should look as if he did. She watched and said nothing. When he was on his knees peering underneath I caught her eye and nodded at the Louis XIV roll-top writing bureau nearer the window. It had a more feminine appeal, with intricate marquetry of floral motifs and arabesques. 'That's the competition,' I said. 'But more expensive.'

She nodded and smiled, but took no step towards it. 'Very elegant.'

Her husband got to his feet, red in the face and breathing heavily. 'Thing is, will it fit? Got a tape measure?'

I began measuring it for him but then it transpired he hadn't pen or paper.

'I can note it on my phone,' she said, opening her handbag.

He shook his head. 'That won't do, I have to write it down.' I handed him my pen and one of my cards. After noting the measurements he studied the card for a long time while holding out the pen for me to take, without looking at me.

'The one in the window is smaller,' his wife said, pointing to the Louis XIV piece. 'Prettier, too.'

He ignored her and turned to me. 'I've another desk where this would go, if it fits. Would you be interested?'

'Not normally, sir, no. But it's possible. It depends on what it is.'

'Just an old desk, nothing special. My father had it, like most of our stuff.'

I looked at her. 'Perhaps you could send me a photo of it?'

'We're not far,' he continued. 'Winchelsea. Come and see it if you like.' He resumed his study of my card. 'Not the same name as the shop. You're not the owner?'

'I am. The shop is long-established, well known under its founder's name, so I kept it.'

'Gold, Simon Gold, Mr Gold. Jewish, I suppose. Must be.' He murmured as if to himself then looked me squarely in the face and laughed. His laugh was abrupt and humourless, like a dog's bark. 'Good name for an antique dealer, Gold.'

I smiled, as always when people made that link. She looked away.

He held out his hand. 'Coombs, Gerald Coombs. Double-o, no e. We'll ring when I've checked the measurements.' His hand felt clammy and passive, like long-dead meat. As he turned away he added, 'If you don't want my desk, I imagine you can do something on the price?'

That should be one of those moments for rapid mental calculation – what did I pay for it, how long have I had it, what are the chances of selling it to anyone else, is this buyer a one-off or might he become a regular customer? But feel and instinct also come into it – is price important to him, will it make the difference between buying and not buying or is haggling just routine, something he always does? Or is it point-scoring, intended to show that he's a canny buyer and nobody's pushover? Or is he showing off in front of his wife, though she had already walked away?

Of course, one always can do something on price, always. That's factored in and it's surprising how few British buyers ever ask. But my hunch with Mr Coombs was that he might respect me for standing firm, that he might even like his desk better the more he paid for it.

'Afraid not, sir,' I said, 'not with that one. It's too special.'

At that moment Stephanie returned carrying a loaf of bread wrapped in white paper which was coming off and trailing behind her. She swept past Mr and Mrs Coombs as if they were not there, obliging them to step aside as she made for the door that leads to our flat upstairs. That was normal for Stephanie when she has anything on her mind, her mind being so constructed as to entertain only one idea at a time. She is my sister and is what used to be called simple; she is a simpleton. Our parents, once they realised she was a few pence short of a shilling, took great trouble to get her diagnosed and to define her place on various spectra, as we now call them. Of course, it was a waste of time and money, not only because her condition never was defined – or rather, it was, several times but each time differently, according to what was fashionable – but because there was nothing to be done about it, whatever you called it. Stephanie is simply Stephanie, that's how she is. Older, cruder terms for people like her are sometimes preferable, I think, not only because they describe behaviour rather than imply knowledge we don't have, but because they imply acceptance. In calling Stephanie simple you are allowing her to be one of us, only less variously capable; but in attempting to pinpoint her on this or that spectrum, to define her by a fancy name, you make her sound different, not quite one of us.

She is Stephanie, she is my sister, she is simple and we have lived together since my divorce. She 'does' for me – that is, she keeps house, to use another unfashionable term – in so far as she can.

She really would not have noticed Mr and Mrs Coombs stepping smartly out of her way that day. I had sent her out with a shopping list which she had put in her pocket and forgotten. Puzzled as to what she should buy, she must have remembered that she often bought bread and so she bought another loaf (to go with the two we already had) and her mind would still have been preoccupied with that when she swept back into the shop. The Coombses must have thought she was rude.

I did not expect to hear from them that day, perhaps not at all – it was Saturday, always busier in terms of footfall in the shop but with fewer serious buyers – and so was surprised when Mr Coombs rang just before I closed. 'Yes? Yes? Who is it?' he said.

I had answered as the shop and had recognised his voice but he seemed to think I had just rung him. 'It's Simon Gold, sir, you—'

'It will fit, that desk. Will fit. We've photographed

the old one but we can't – Charlotte can't – seem to send it. We're not very good with electronic contraptions.' He barked his laugh again. 'Couldn't pop over and have a peek at it, could you? Just a peek. We're only in Winchelsea, won't take you five minutes. Have a drink.'

Theirs was one of the white weather-boarded houses in that ancient hill town, set back from the junction of two quiet roads, with a spacious garden and a garage. Heels sounded on the parquet hall floor when I knocked and Mrs Coombs answered. She had changed from the jeans and jumper of the early afternoon to a dark skirt and white blouse, a solitary diamond on a fine gold chain around her neck, on one wrist a slim gold watch, on the other a slim gold bracelet. Her light-brown hair looked freshly washed and she wore make-up and pale lipstick.

As we shook hands I noticed hers were large and bony, quite out of keeping with the rest of her. It was as if someone else's had been grafted on – her father's, perhaps – and for one mad moment I almost commented on them. 'I'm sorry, you must be going out. Should I come another time?'

She pulled a face and smiled. 'Golf club dinner. No rush. Gerald is expecting you. He's very excited.'

As before, I noticed how her smile deepened the lines and wrinkles around her lips and eyes. But these very marks of decay and the valiant, unavailing, daily struggle against them are to me endearing. The way women – it's usually women – struggle to keep up appearances seems to me not only a matter of vanity but a courageous assertion of the human spirit against the inevitable. She had – has – a pretty face with small regular features and those misty blue eyes. I imagined her staring every morning in the mirror at the encroaching ruin, before bravely renewing the struggle. At least she had the good sense never to have a face-lift or anything like that; better a dignified, gradual acceptance.

Yet those hands – she must have been conscious of them since childhood, wondering at them, regretting them, hiding them. I was already in love with her for her flaws, almost.

She led me across the hall into a drawing room crowded with heavy old dark furniture, the sort that for years now has been hard to sell. The walls were cluttered with portraits of bewhiskered military gentlemen and ladies with long dresses who looked as if they worried about constipation. I followed her through a door at the far end into a study overlooking an immaculate back garden. The walls of this room were mostly lined with books, some with leather bindings, the rest old hardbacks. Mr Coombs was reading at a desk in an alcove to one side of the fireplace.

'Darling, here's Mr Gold.'

'Ah, Mr Gold.' He seemed well able to contain his excitement, barely turning his head and pushing his swivel chair back with his foot as he slowly got up. He wore a greenish tweed suit and the local golf club tie with a tie-pin. There was no handshaking and he looked at me as if struggling to remember who I was. 'What can I do for you?'

'He's come to see the desk, darling.'

'Of course, the desk.' He stood back and pointed at it. 'This is where it will go, in this alcove, you see. The measurements fit and it won't project so far into the room as this one. And I can pull the top down, shut away all my papers and what-have-you. Thing is, can you do anything with this one?'

The existing desk did indeed project inconveniently into the room. It was a handsome pedestal piece, a partners' desk. Yew, I guessed, with a fine grey-blue leather top.

'Came from my father's office when he retired. Solicitor in Ashford, senior partner. Too good to throw away but too big for this room. Too big for most rooms these days, I suppose you'll tell me?'

'Indeed, sir, but there's a home for everything some-where.' I examined all I could see of it. It was a Bevan Funnell, one of their quality 1950s reproductions, and none the worse for that. It differed from others in having marquetry around the drawer handles. I had never seen that on a Bevan Funnell.

'Any good to you?' he asked. 'Can you sell it?'

It would have been easy to look sorrowful and point out that not only was it too large for most modern homes but that it was a fifties repro, thus not an original antique like the one he wanted to buy. I could offer to send my delivery chaps round to take it off his hands for a few hundred if he couldn't find a home for it himself, then send it to auction and pocket the profit. I didn't have to tell him that it was actually worth more than the Edwardian roll-top he was buying.

His plump pink jowls, his curiously expressionless brown eyes and his ample stomach all contributed to his aura of bovine complacency; but there was something else, too, a kind of passivity that suggested something missing rather than a calm temperament. You couldn't quite trust it, as if he might change at any moment.

I could have taken the desk from him without compunction but it was not business I was thinking of as I regarded him. It was the thought of her having to climb into bed alongside him every night, of having to live with him all day, of feeling superfluous, frequently ignored and as frequently depended upon. Thus, instead of being businesslike, I said, 'To be honest, Mr Coombs, although it's a modern reproduction it was made by one of the best-known furniture makers of the last century and is not only very good but very unusual. I've never seen another like it. It could fetch more at auction than the one you're buying and so it would be less than honest of me to quote you a part-exchange price. Your father had good taste.'

There was a long pause. He remained perfectly still, looking at me as if waiting for me to continue. Eventually, he said, 'Take it and sell it for me? Take a cut?'

We shook on it, his hand as limp and clammy as before. 'You have some nice bits and pieces here,' I continued as we walked back into the drawing room. Mrs Coombs had disappeared.

He looked indifferently, almost morosely, at the Chesterfield sofa, the matching pair of high-backed chairs that looked like restored seventeenth-century pieces but may have been Victorian copies, the elegant Georgian sidetables, the two small occasional chairs, the ancestral portraits. 'All from my father, keen on family stuff. Loved it. No good for most people these days, no good for us either, really. No family, can't get rid of it, nowhere else to put it.'

'Are all these your ancestors?'

He surveyed the portraits as if they were a mob of unwelcome visitors. 'Military lot, as you can see. Army or law. Mostly lawyers, the earlier ones. Bloody lawyers. I was neither, of course.'

The 'of course' was interesting, though I wasn't sure what it said about him. The subjects were mostly nineteenth-century figures in various martial poses, plus a few rather solemn married couples in eighteenth-century costumes and the stiffly posed single ladies I had noticed earlier. At the far end of the room was a smaller, darker painting of a man with long hair and plain brown clothes. 'He looks like a preacher,' I said.

'Preacher or lawyer, maybe both, can't remember. Civil War, anyway. They go back much earlier, the family. No older portraits, though. That's the oldest. All from Warwickshire or Worcestershire.'

On the wall above the fireplace were three swords, hung horizontally. 'Ancestral swords, too?' I asked.

'Ancestral everything. All ancestral here.'

The top and bottom ones looked like conventional nineteenth-century cavalry swords. The centre one was different, possibly a Civil War period mortuary sword, as they became known. I was tempted to examine it but didn't want to appear too inquisitive and anyway he was moving towards the door. Then I noticed another. 'That one too?'

There was a fourth sword lying in the hearth at my feet between two pokers and a small shovel, its hilt resting on the stone edge. It was older, longer and narrower than those hanging above, a rapier rather than a cut-and-thrust fighting weapon. It was also in much worse condition, dirty, the blade blackened by fire and smoke, the hilt and pommel bashed about. There was no shine and it was impossible to see any detailing.

Mr Coombs turned, his dark eyes reluctantly

following my finger. 'That? That's my poker. Longer than the others, long enough for me to poke the fire without getting out of my chair. No good for anything else, too far gone to hang on the wall. Want a drink?'

He didn't sound as if he wanted me to accept. 'That's very kind but you're about to go out, aren't you? Next time, perhaps, when we've sorted out the desks.'

He turned again and left the room. By the time I reached the hall he was already at the door and holding it open for me. 'Let me know when it's coming,' he said. 'Give you a cheque then.'

As I walked down the pebble path the door closed behind me and I heard him shout, 'You ready?'

Chapter Two

I close the shop on Sundays. Most antique dealers stay open for the weekend tourist pilgrimage but my experience, perhaps because I'm at the more expensive end of the local market, is that Sunday window-shoppers are even less likely to open their wallets than their Saturday counterparts. On Mondays, when other dealers usually close, I occasionally get serious buyers.

Sunday mornings I spend at my desk in the shop, seeing to accounts and administration and scanning the on-screen market while Stephanie vacuums and cleans the flat upstairs. I don't let her do it during the week because, as with most old buildings, there's no soundproofing and the hoover sounds as if it's coming through the floor. I say 'let her' because cleaning the flat is the highlight of her week. She has a routine I taught her after my wife left and I had rescued her from the sheltered housing she had been in since our parents died. She loves her routine, adhering scrupulously to it and taking great pleasure in walking me round afterwards to show me everything she's done. She relishes inspection and approval. Afterwards we get in the car and drive off somewhere for a pub lunch followed by a walk. Her favourite is a walk by the sea, when she laughs out loud at the waves and clings to my arm like a toddler, though she's older than me.

It was on that Sunday evening when Stephanie was watching snooker on television – she loves that too, without understanding it, I think because of the very green sward and the moving coloured balls – that the connection suddenly coalesced in my mind. I had been thinking off and on of Mrs Coombs, assuming she led a wretched life with her husband and idly imagining how it would be transformed if she lived with someone presentable and reasonable, as I then believed myself to be. Not that I had any intention of bringing about such a state of affairs.

At the same time my unconscious must have been working towards a hypothetical conclusion that my conscious mind, when presented with it, was only too willing to accept as fact. Or possible fact. From the moment it occurred the thought preoccupied me day and night. It still does, albeit no longer in its original purity and interwoven now with unforeseen consequences. Gerald Coombs's emphasis on the spelling of his name – double-o, no e, he insisted – must have germinated in the yeast of my unconscious until it became what it always had the potential to be. Also in that yeast must have been fragments of a recent television programme about Shakespeare's life and the memory of a phrase from his will I had once read in a biography. It was late in the evening when the mixture fermented. For some moments after it struck me I remained in my armchair, book in hand, asking myself whether I remembered or imagined the wording of the will. Then I went back downstairs to the shop and opened up the computer (I've still not got round to a laptop and tend to use my phone only as a phone). And there it was, in black and white in Shakespeare's will, among the lesser bequests: 'To Mr Thomas Combe my Sword.'

That phrase, Gerald Coombs's name, his accumulation of ancestral possessions, his seventeenth-century family, their Warwickshire origins, that blackened and battered old sword in the hearth – it could all be coincidence. Things are, more often than not. But was it possible, just possible, that Gerald Coombs's poker could – just possibly could – be Shakespeare's sword?

Professional deformity – more kindly termed interest – meant that the bequests in Shakespeare's will that stuck in my mind were those concerning items of furniture or adornment. Most famously, of course, he left his wife the 'second best bed with the furniture' and his daughter Judith 'my broad silver gilt bole'. The bulk of his bequests were property and money which went to his favoured daughter Susanna and her husband, along with frustratingly unspecified 'goodes, chattels leases plate jewels & household stuff whatsoever'.

But the image of the sword had always stood out for me, shimmering across the darkening fields of memory. I know a little about swords, though I'm no authority, and I often used to wonder what sort it was, why he had it, where he got it, why Thomas Combe and, above all, what happened to it. Could it still exist, unrecognised in some attic or indifferently displayed with a few Elizabethan daggers in some museum? Or used as a poker by a man who couldn't be bothered to get out of his chair?

The key was to establish whether Thomas Combe could be an ancestor of Gerald Coombs. No double-o, of course, and Thomas did have an e, but spelling varies with times and places and Gerald had mentioned ancestors of roughly the right period and location. If any of them were Stratford men, and Thomas was a Stratford man, that would greatly increase the likelihood.

I researched far into the night. Gratifyingly, others had done the hard slog before me. Thomas Combe was indeed a Stratford man and a lawyer. He was younger than Shakespeare – twenty-seven when Shakespeare died in 1616 aged fifty-two – and had a brother and great-uncle who were also lawyers. 'Mostly lawyers ... bloody lawyers,' Gerald had said. Shakespeare had bought land from them – 107 acres, no small amount – and there seem to have been property dealings between Thomas's father and Shakespeare's father. Clearly, they all knew each other, certainly through business and possibly friendship. Leaving the sword – expensive and often treasured items – to young Thomas must surely have been a mark of friendship or gratitude.

Thomas himself was admitted to Middle Temple in 1608 when he must have been about nineteen. After that he returned to practise in Stratford, was made Recorder in 1648 and remained in that post until his death in 1657, aged sixty-eight. A good age for those days, meaning he lived through the Civil War. I assumed he was a Cromwellian since Warwickshire was strongly Puritan – even in Shakespeare's lifetime the corporation of Stratford forbade plays in the Guildhall – and his cousin was granted land seized from the Royalist Bishop of Worcester. He helped organise and control repairs to the Stratford parish church. His step-sister, Bridget, married a future Governor of Connecticut but Thomas appears never to have married and died without issue, leaving the bulk of his estate to Warwickshire cousins. The sword is not mentioned in his will but, assuming he still had it, it would have gone to his cousin William Combe of nearby Alvechurch, to whom he left all his goods and chattels. And so it disappears from history.

As does Thomas. Were it not for those six words in Shakespeare's will we should have known nothing of him or the sword. He would have been swallowed by the great maw of time and the world would very soon be as if he had never been, once the temporary ripple among family and friends had subsided. Of course, he would never have guessed that he would be a subject of interest four hundred years on; if he had it would have felt like a kind of immortality, spurious but still desirable.

These might seem morbid reflections for a middle-aged man alone at night in his shop, illuminated by desk lamp and screen, surrounded by dead people's possessions. But I felt far from morbid. Things outlive us, which is partly why I like them. The pen I was using to take notes, a 1920s Conway Stewart, was made long before I was born and will function for someone long after I have disappeared. Things speak to us of lives past, evidence not of immortality but of the fact that not everything is as transient as ourselves. That's why the thought of Shakespeare's sword cheered and excited me, filling me with energy. If it could be plucked out of the great maw it would bring us, in a very small way, closer to Shakespeare, to Thomas Combe and to all those other forgotten Combes who had owned and handled it, all the way down to Gerald. The Combes – or Coombses – would end with him, I guessed. But the sword would go on. It could also be worth a lot of money.

*

On the Monday morning I rang the chaps who do the heavy lifting for me, a couple of lads with a van – or rather, a succession of vans since none seems to last long. They're a scruffy pair and a good example of how you can't always judge by appearances since they're punctual and polite and take care not to damage things. That's why I pay them a bit over the odds for our part of the world. They live on a caravan site along the coast at Camber where they seem to be involved in multifarious enterprises of, I suspect, uncertain legality.

I then rang the Coombses. Eventually, as I was holding my breath to leave a message, Gerald answered. That is, there was a sigh he made no attempt to conceal and then the single, tired word, 'Well?' It appeared that any intrusion from the outside world was not only unwelcome but not worth bothering with. However, a trace of animation entered his voice when I said I was ringing to see whether that afternoon was a good time for my chaps to deliver the desk.

'Can't see anything wrong with it,' he said cautiously, as if inspecting an intricate piece of machinery. 'Nothing much wrong with that. Shan't be here myself but Charlotte will let them in.'

'They'll take your old desk straight to the auction rooms at Lewes. It may be in time for the next auction, depending how much they've got.' There was no response. I decided to construe silence as consent and took a chance. 'Nothing else I can take for you, I suppose? While my chaps are there. Any old bits and pieces you no longer want?'

The silence continued, long enough for me to fear I'd offended him. Then he said, 'Clear the bloody house for all I care.'

I affected a laugh, unreciprocated. 'Would three o'clock be all right for Mrs Coombs?' But it was too late; he had put the phone down.

I closed the shop after lunch. Stephanie knew the heavy lifters and could be trusted to let them in and show them which desk, though I left a note on it in case anything unexpected threw her. I drove over to Winchelsea about half an hour before the lifters were due. Charlotte raised her eyebrows when she saw it was me, I hoped with pleasurable surprise though it might have been quizzical. 'Thought I'd better see that my chaps get it right,' I said. 'Not that they don't normally.'

'That's very kind of you. May I get you some tea or coffee?'

'Tea would be very nice.'

She was wearing jeans with the jumper she had worn in the shop on Saturday. I stood watching her in the kitchen as she made the tea. Her movements were precise and considered, almost as if she were performing surgery. Or as if, conscious of her oversized hands, she felt she had to make a point of delicacy.

'What a lovely light kitchen.' My flat was small-windowed and dark, like most old houses. This led to a discussion of the house and eventually a tour. It was one of the relatively few detached houses in Winchelsea, larger inside than it looked from without. From the two rear bedrooms we could see the sea. 'That's what's frustrating about my flat,' I told her. 'So near the sea but we can't see it because it's blocked by the other side of the street. They have a good view of it from the back but we get no benefit at all. We get the gulls, though. Wretched creatures.'

Her expression was extravagantly sympathetic, as if I'd announced an amputation rather than an inconvenience. 'Oh dear, how awful for you. We get them too, they make such a dreadful racket especially first thing in the morning. But probably not as badly as you. They sound louder in towns, with all the reverberation.'

Upstairs was as crammed with old paintings and furniture as downstairs. It wasn't a treasure trove – there were some nice pieces but most of it was simply old, as if an undiscriminating dealer had retired without clearing his stock. But on the landing was a long-case clock which I knew to be both rare and not worth much. The polished oak case had probably once housed a finer clock; the face, plain enamel with Arabic numerals, was friendly rather than smart, showing hours, minutes and dates, the latter through a downturned mouth. There was some faded floral decoration, green, yellow and gold, in the corners. It was stopped at ten to four and was interesting only because it was a local clock, by H. Bourn of Rye. I knew a little about Mr Bourn. His dates were 1801–38 and he ceased trading in 1837. He may have begun as a blacksmith who graduated to clock-making. There were two other examples of his work, one owned by a lady in Tenterden and another by a former mayor of Rye who used to keep it in the mayoral office and removed it when he left. They were simple clocks, weight-driven with thirty-hour movements and anchor escapements, but they worked. They were of no value to horologists or to the trade in general; their appeal was strictly local, and to only a few at that.

She noticed me looking at it. 'It was working only he – Gerald – stopped winding it because the chimes kept him awake. He doesn't sleep as well as he used to.'

'Did they keep you awake too?'

'Of course they did, for years. But I didn't feel I could say anything.' She smiled.

'Tell him it's no trouble to disconnect the chime, if he wants. It would go for longer without winding then. I could do it in a couple of minutes.'

'Could you, could you really?' Her eyes widened as if I'd announced the discovery of a miracle cure. 'That would be wonderful. So very kind of you. I'll tell him, I'll certainly tell him, yes.'

We stood facing each other. She had one thing in

common with her husband: pauses that were discon-
certingly long, making it hard to know whether she
was collecting her thoughts, or politely allowing time
for a response, or was simply unaware. Because they
made me feel awkward, it soon became my practice to
fill them. That was a mistake, a sign of weakness. 'You
sound as if you don't expect him to do anything about
it.' I imagined Mr Coombs grunting acknowledgement
of my offer and leaving it at that.

'Exactly, quite right, how perceptive of you. This
was his parents' house, you see. He was brought up
here. These – all this furniture – were all their things
that came down through the family on his father's side.
There's practically nothing of his mother's. He com-
plains about it all the time, says we're too cluttered,
which we are, and that we live under the dead hand of
the past, which we do, but he won't do anything about
it. Nothing must be changed. It's a burden to – to both
of us, really. We just go on.'

'But he's getting rid of his father's desk downstairs
and buying a new one.'

She clasped her hands, pressing them against her
stomach. 'That's so unusual, yes, took me completely
by surprise. I didn't say anything because – well, I
don't want to discourage change.' She laughed. 'But
I'm surprised he's gone through with it. Maybe it
doesn't count in his eyes because it hasn't been handed
down through the centuries, it was just something his

father bought for his office and brought home with him. Do you see what I mean? Do you see?'

Her eyes were almost violet in that light and her appeal gratuitously urgent. I nodded, which felt like an inadequate response. Then, after another pause, she turned and headed downstairs. Throughout our conversation the image of the sword in the hearth hovered in my mind like an alcoholic's knowledge of a hidden bottle. I was considering how to mention it when the doorbell rang.

The desks were safely exchanged during ten or so brisk minutes as my chaps made light work of the lifting while offering their opinions of the weather, the house, the pot-holed East Sussex roads and the state of the nation. Mrs Coombs fluttered about, extravagantly grateful. It would have been natural for me to leave with them, of course, but I deliberately remained in the study, contemplating the desk. 'It looks right in that spot.'

She shrugged. Her manner had changed when she closed the door on my chaps, as if she were deflated. 'It's where he wants it.'

'It protrudes less into the room than the other one.'

'Yes.'

Another pause was coming. I was about to ask whether I could examine the sword when she brightened and said, 'Would you like another cup of tea?'

'That's very kind. Only if you've time.' I followed

her back into the drawing room, pausing by the fire-place as if on impulse. 'May I have a quick look at these swords?'

'Of course. Milk, no sugar, wasn't it?' She crossed the hall into the kitchen.

For appearance's sake, I unhooked the middle one from the wall. As I had suspected, it was a seventeenth-century piece, a well-preserved broadsword of the Civil War period. The blade was engraved with ME FECIT HOVSLOE – the village of Hounslow having become a centre of sword-making by then – and it had a dish-shaped guard with two knuckle guards screwed into the pommel. It was the Victorians who called them mortuary swords, wrongly assuming that the stylised human heads chiselled into their hilts represented the executed Charles I and his queen, Henrietta, hence that the owners were Royalists. But in fact the two heads were merely contemporary fashion and such swords were used by both sides. I didn't bother to examine the nineteenth-century military swords hang-ing above and below it.

The kettle was already boiling in the kitchen and there was a clatter of cups and saucers. I laid down the mortuary sword and took up the one in the hearth, my heart beating as if I were already stealing it. It was a rapier, that was already obvious, longer than the mor-tuary sword, a pointed, double-edged weapon intended for duelling or self-defence or stealthy murder rather than battle, designed to be worn with a cloak, a mark of status. Exactly what one would have expected of a man as desirous for status as William Shakespeare.

The blade was blackened by fire and smoke and no maker's mark was visible. It had no fuller – a groove in the blade designed to reduce weight – but instead had a ridge or spine that strengthened it, making the blade triangular in cross-section. It was known as a hollow ground ridge, I had read, the sides ground out or scalloped to save weight. That was expensive and time-consuming work, suggesting quality steel and a top-notch product. It was long, too, between three and a half and four feet plus the hilt, grip and ovoid pommel, so clearly made before the later fashion for shorter blades. The hilt was almost as blackened as the blade although I could make out some sort of decoration or adornment beneath the dirt. The pommel was large and heavy, partly to balance that long blade and partly, we know from illustrations, because at close quarters it was useful for literally pommelling your opponent's skull. There was also a cross-guard – a slim metal bar at right angles to the grip, in this case downturned at one end like a swan's head – and a curved knuckle guard or bow. The grip felt as if there were coiled wire beneath the dirt.

I stood holding it for I don't know how long, pointing it at the fireplace and thinking – could it, could it really be? Could I be holding what Shakespeare's hand had held? And if so could there be a dimension unknown to us through which I might absorb or sense something – anything – of him? There ought to be, given the almost daily revelations of counter-intuitive truths from particle physics. The longer I held the sword the more convinced I became that there was something, that eventually one would feel it and that this, surely, must have been Shakespeare's sword. The Combe-Coombs name, their accumulated inheritance, their legal antecedents and geographical origins, made coincidence recede in my mind.

'I hope I haven't made it too weak.' This time she brought the tea on a polished wooden tray, with a plate of ginger biscuits. 'No custard creams, I'm afraid. Gerald must have finished them all and they seem to be harder to find now.'

'He likes his custard creams?'

'Yes, a life-long passion. Not that he's generally . . .' She half-hid her smile as she lowered the tray onto one of the sidetables by the armchairs. 'Are you interested in swords, Mr . . . Mr Gold?'

'Interested and I know a bit about them but I'm no expert. They're not an obsession, I'm afraid.'

She smiled again at that. 'Gerald thinks those on the wall might be quite valuable. One was used by one of his ancestors in the Civil War, he thinks.'

I was reluctant to let go of the rapier so picked up the mortuary sword with my left hand. 'That would be this one. It's certainly of that period and is in very good condition.

'Dreadful to think it might have killed people.'

'Yes.' The thought that a weapon might have killed actually enhanced its appeal to me, but that was a reaction I had learned to conceal. Personally, I had always rather liked the idea of killing someone. Not someone I hated or feared – my motive was not polluted by any personal consideration. No, it was purer and worse than that: narcissism. I just wanted to know what it felt like. Concealing such thoughts from Mrs Coombs was, I later discovered, unnecessary.

She picked up her tea and sat in one of the armchairs. I carefully replaced the rapier in the hearth and restored the mortuary sword to its place on the wall between the others, then sat in the other chair. It felt awkward, sitting side by side drinking tea, facing the empty fireplace with, to its side, the blank television screen. 'And the other one?' I asked. 'The one used as a poker? Did that belong to a Coombs ancestor too?' Absurdly, I could feel my heart beating again.

She glanced at it and shrugged. 'Presumably. I've never heard him say anything about that one.'

'It might be worth cleaning it up a little and having a look. Swords sometimes tell you something about themselves – makers' marks and so on.'

'I can't imagine Gerald getting round to cleaning anything. Unless it's to do with golf.'

'Strange to be surrounded by so much ancestry and to have no interest in it.'

'Yet at the same time he refuses to get rid of any of it, as I was saying. Despite the fact that he's always moaning about it and every now and again threatens to dump it all.'

'I could clean it up for you, that sword.'

Once again her expression was radiant with implausibly extravagant gratitude. 'That's so sweet of you, Mr Gold, but there's no need, there really isn't. Have another biscuit.'

We moved on to the pleasures and pains of living in a very small, very quiet and very ancient town, until I felt that conversation was becoming an effort for us both. I stood, saying I had better get back to the shop.

'There's no one to look after it when you're not there? I assumed that lady who came in when we were leaving . . .'

I told her about Stephanie, going on for some time when I saw the sympathy in her face.

'Not many brothers – not many men – would do what you're doing,' she said as we lingered by the front door.

'Can't not, really, no choice,' I said breezily, with what was meant to come across as selfless good cheer. 'Anyway, it's not as if I have anyone else to look after.'

'You've no family, no wife or children?'

'Divorced before we had children. Probably as well. You and Mr Coombs . . .?'

'We have no children.'

It felt as if neither of us wanted to part, but it was becoming awkward not to. I was outside now, hesitating on the path. 'Nor siblings? So the family will end with—?'

'I'm afraid so.'

'But not for a while yet, we hope.' I smiled and then tried to look as if I'd just thought of something. 'Talking of family, names and so on, has it always been spelled Coombs?'

She looked puzzled. 'I don't know, I think so. I'll ask – actually, no, I think on some of the old portraits – have you got another moment? I'm not keeping you?'

The bewhiskered Waterloo hero in the hall was a Coombs, as was one of his eighteenth-century ancestors in the drawing room. Another was unnamed, though there was a facial resemblance, but the seventeenth-century Puritan civilian at the far end of the room was a Combe, William Combe.

'This is the one I was thinking of,' she said. 'Does this mean he's not really a Coombs?'

'Not at all, it's all quite consistent. Before standardised spelling and registration of births, deaths and marriages, voters lists and whatever, spellings frequently changed. People sometimes even spelled their own names differently at different times – those that could spell at all, that is. Shakespeare's will, for instance, has him as both S-h-a-c-k-s-p-e-a-r-e and S-h-a-c-k-s-p-a-r-e.'

She looked at me as if I'd announced something sensational. 'Really? Really? I didn't know.'

I regretted it immediately. I'd mentioned Shakespeare because he was so much on my mind but I didn't want her to realise that. Still less did I want her to take an interest in his will. 'Not just Shakespeare, of course. I've read no end of old wills with similar inconsistencies, sometimes perpetrated by the people themselves but often through careless transcription by clerks. It extends well into the nineteenth century. You'd probably find similar confusions now with the names of immigrants.'

'How astonishing.'

'When this portrait was painted variation was the norm rather than the exception. Also, people sometimes changed name spellings for social reasons, one version being thought of as smarter than another, especially if it coincided with an aristocratic version. Sometimes they changed their names completely in order to inherit or be associated with a distinguished ancestor or relative. Oliver Cromwell's family adopted Cromwell in order to make their association with Thomas Cromwell, Henry VIII's chief minister, closer than it was.'

Or so I'd read. I couldn't remember where. Nor could I remember what Oliver's family was previously called. Happily, she was too busy gushing with admiration to press for details. We moved back towards the door and repeated an abbreviated version of my earlier leave-taking.

As soon as I got back I began tracking down the Cromwell family's previous name. There was no need, no one was going to ask me. I suspected Mrs Coombs had no more intellectual curiosity than most people one meets. I didn't blame her for it, any more than I blamed the mass of humanity for lacking interest in anything beyond their immediate concerns. It may depress the altruist but it's what helped us to evolve, it's what we're like. Nor do I except myself from this; it's just that, having remembered something like the Cromwell example and then committed myself publicly to it, I couldn't rest until I'd settled it. The family's previous name was Williams; they were descended from Thomas Cromwell's married sister, Katherine. I would tell that to Mrs Coombs one day, whether she wanted to know or not.

Not that I was going to rest that evening, anyway. It and the evenings to come were largely taken up with researches into Thomas Combe, Elizabethan swords and Shakespeare himself. I soon found not one but three William Combes related to Thomas. There was his elder brother, another lawyer who was twice Sheriff of Stratford, an aggressive man with a chequered financial history. In 1614 he provoked a legal dispute peripherally involving Shakespeare. He enclosed common land without going through the proper procedures, making no secret of his intention to sell for a profit. The dispute, which included physical intimidation, went on until 1619 when the Privy Council ordered him to restore the land to the village. There's no record of whether or not he did. An example of how vice is rewarded, he outlived his younger brother, Thomas, dying in 1667 and leaving his substantial property to his grandson, Sir Combe Wagstaff. It subsequently went to the better-known Clopton family.

But of the sword there is no mention, which is puzzling because swords were expensive and often valued by families. If Shakespeare had had his made for him it would surely have been a significant heirloom, like the 'broad silver-gilt bole' he left to his less-favoured daughter, Judith. His leaving the sword to Thomas – he had no son to inherit, young Hamnet having died – must surely have been a mark of favour and distinction. Did Thomas not value it, or had he given it away, or was it somehow taken up for service in the Civil War?

Though almost certain it would have been a rapier, I searched for any indication of what kind of sword it was, why Shakespeare had it, whether he ever used it. It's conceivable that it was for self-protection. He knew fellow playwrights and actors who had fought and killed with swords; Ben Jonson killed the actor Gabriel Spencer and possibly also another man in a duel in the Low Countries, while Christopher Marlowe, notorious for 'causing sudden privy injuries to men', was killed by a knife. London's South Bank, where Shakespeare mostly worked and to which he would have walked daily from his lodgings in Cripplegate, was known for violence and disorder. His journeys to and from Stratford might have been vulnerable to highwaymen.

But Shakespeare was no fighting man. It's more likely that he acquired his sword as a result of his successful 1596 application for a coat of arms. The grant by the College of Heralds of a coat of arms gentrified the holder and his family – a number of later documents refer to Shakespeare as Gentleman or Gent. – and also conferred the right to bear a sword in public. Outward signs of status mattered to ambitious, upwardly mobile Elizabethan families, and Shakespeare's was no exception. His father, John, had tried unsuccessfully for a coat of arms in the 1560s or 1570s but lived to see his son achieve it. Perhaps Shakespeare sought it partly on his father's behalf. Family status mattered enough to him for him subsequently to apply to quarter the arms – that is, divide the shield – with those of his mother's family, the older and more distinguished Ardens. This was no small business – the thirty-guinea fee was more than the Stratford schoolmaster would have earned in a year and Shakespeare had to call in aid his father's service as Bailiff of Stratford and his great-grandfather's military service for Henry VII. Once granted, John Shakespeare and his descendants were entitled to display the coat of arms on their door and on all their possessions.

Such marks of respectability would have been particularly important to anyone in Shakespeare's profession. Actors and theatres were far from respectable, being associated with disorder, drunkenness and whoring. It may even be that he was mocked for his pains by Jonson, his friend and rival, who wrote of players with social aspirations: 'They forget they are i' the statute, the rascals, they are blazoned there, there they are tricked, they and their pedigrees: they need no other heralds.' But for the son of a provincial glove-maker who had made himself playwright, actor-manager and part owner of a company that played at court by royal command and later had minor roles in state occasions as grooms of the bedchamber with their own issue of red cloth, it would have been worth the mockery to have been accorded the status of William Shakespeare, Gent. Just as Gerald Coombs, perhaps, had been pleased to be elected to his golf club. Such vanities, unlike the aggressive assertion of ego, are mostly harmless.

If my surmise were correct, then Shakespeare's sword would most likely have been a fashionable rapier like the one in the Coombses' hearth. It would not have been a war-fighting sword, broad-bladed and designed for slashing, awkward to wear with civilian clothing. The rapier – though Gerald's example was heavier than I had expected –was more elegant, signifying the rank and wealth to which Shakespeare aspired. The word rapier, I read, derived from the Spanish *espada ropera*, meaning sword of the robes, something you could wear with court dress. But it was still a deadly weapon with a long reach, slim and piercing sharp, first choice for duellists and probably a deterrent to assailants armed only with knife or club.

As to the coat of arms itself, little is known. There are two rough drafts of a document in which the Garter King-of-Arms declares he has assigned and confirmed a shield 'Gold, on a bend sables, a spear of the first steeled argent, and for his crest or cognisance a falcon, his wings displayed argent, standing on a wreath of his colours, supporting a spear gold, steeled as aforesaid, set upon a helmet with mantles and tassels as hath been accustomed and doth more plainly appear depicted on this argent.' There is a rough draft of a simplified version and three drafts of a possible motto, 'Not Without Right'. No fair copy has ever come to light, nor any full illustration. Nor is it known whether Shakespeare or his father put it on the front door in Stratford or on any possessions. Among the latter I wondered whether he might conceivably have had a simplified version engraved on his sword, beneath all that dirt and discoloration. But that would have been unusual.

Frankly, such heraldic details bore me, partly because of the effort of interpretation and partly because – well, so what? They flatter the vanity of the owner, harmlessly enough, and doubtless interest those that follow such things. Just like personalised car number plates, for those who can be bothered with them. Nevertheless, I did take the trouble to look online at the Royal Shakespeare Theatre's worked-up version in glass of the coat of arms, based on the description. I was looking at this in the shop that evening when Stephanie crept down and stood behind me, unnoticed.

'That's pretty,' she said.

She likes obvious colours and 'pretty' is her all-purpose word for anything visually appealing. I enlarged it for her.

'What is it?' she asked.

The explanation took a while. How good a job I made of it was evident when she said she wanted a coat like that. It is never easy to divert Stephanie once she starts on something. Her mind is single-track and she persists with the doggedness of a terrier at a rat-hole. It can go on for days. Anxious to close this track down before it really got going, I turned off the computer and stood. 'Time we went to bed, I think.'

I had to move aside because Stephanie did not step back to make room for me. She often stands too close to people, unaware of the conventions of distance. This time her abstracted but concentrated gaze at the blank screen indicated that she was thinking about something. She could be upset if roused too abruptly from such states. I waited a few more seconds, then said gently, 'Come on now, Steph, time for bed.'

'He rang.' Her eyes were still on the keyboard.

'Who rang?'

'The man.'

It was important to proceed gently. Any hint of impatience could reduce her to stammering incoherence, with trembling lips and wide, frightened eyes. And no answer. 'Did he? That's interesting. Which man was it? Can you remember?'

'The man who was here.' She paused. 'With the lady.'

Two or three couples had been in since the Coombses but they were the only ones likely to have rung. 'What did he say?' No answer. 'Have a think, see if you can remember.'

'He wants the desk.'

'The desk that was in the window? The one he's bought?'

'Back. He wants you to bring it back.'

'Thank you, Steph, that's very helpful. I'll ring him. Did he leave his name – did he say who he was?'

She turned from the screen and faced me now. 'The man with the lady, the lady you like.'

That was typical of Stephanie. Great swathes of life pass her by, people, places, episodes flow unnoticed around her, but then she picks on some detail, some remark or, as in this case, some inclination I was unaware I had betrayed. She had returned to the shop as the Coombses were leaving, had given no sign of having noticed them at all, I wasn't sure I'd even spoken to them in her hearing, unless on the phone to Mrs Coombs; but something about me, something of my manner, had told her. She couldn't have described the desk, the transaction, the Coombses themselves but, like Archilochus' hedgehog, she knew one big thing.

When I rang them the next morning I got Mrs Coombs, who cut me off before I had finished introducing myself. 'Yes, hello, yes, I'll get him, he's just here.' There was a pause which became an interlude until eventually the muffled voices ceased and she returned. 'He's going to come in and see you this morning.'

'Is there a problem with the desk, anything I can—'

'Gerald will see you. He wants to see you. Lovely to speak. Bye.'

The morning was otherwise uneventful. It was raining and there were few shoppers about, not even any pretended window-shoppers seeking shelter. I dealt with a few online enquiries and otherwise spent more time than I should have standing just back from the window with coffee cup and saucer, watching the rain on the cobbles. I find rain refreshing rather than depressing, perhaps because there's something happening. I had set Stephanie to polishing some of the silver pieces in the back room. She likes tasks like that, albeit she's very slow and you can't trust her not to lose smaller pieces, so I'm careful with what I give her. As for weather, I don't think she notices it at all. Left to herself, her dress takes no account of it and I often have to choose for her or suggest to her. I'm not particularly good at women's clothes and I suspect she may seem oddly dressed to most people; but, then, she is odd. She notices bright colours, though, and would go on wearing the same pink, red or blue thing forever if I didn't intervene. Whatever goes on inside her head – there's always something going on – must be wholly absorbing, rendering her oblivious to the myriad distractions most of us are prey to.

It was lunchtime and I was about to suggest she went upstairs and put some bread in the toaster when Gerald Coombs arrived. He must have walked briskly from around the corner because I had no warning until the doorway was filled by a great black umbrella. He managed to open the door but struggled to collapse the umbrella completely, showering rain onto my polished oak floorboards. When he did finally collapse it he brought it down like a sabre-swipe from a raised position, this time showering me as I reached to close the door. His cheeks were red with effort and indignation.

'There you are!' he almost shouted. 'The man I wanted. I've come to see you.' He strode into the middle of the shop and turned to face me. His umbrella began a small puddle and he seemed oblivious of the raindrops on his heavy black spectacles. 'It's no good, it won't do! I can't part with my inheritance just like that, even if it was brought in and not passed down. I don't know what you were thinking of, what you take me for. I can't dump my inheritance like so much junk, it's part of me, what I am. I'd be betraying them all, all my ancestors, my family, if I got rid of it. I must have it back. D'you see? D'you see that, eh?'

'You want your desk back, sir?' It was a lame response but he was in such a lather that I felt it necessary to be very precise, in case he was confused as well.

'Of course I do, what else would I be talking about? Don't know what came over me to think of getting rid of it. It was her influence, she hates it all, hates me, has no feeling for any of it. Wouldn't have come near this wretched place if it wasn't for her. Would I, eh?'

That wasn't at all how I recalled it but the priority was to humour him. As ill-luck would have it, a thirty-something couple were hovering outside as if about to enter. 'The desk went to the auction house, as you may recall, Mr Coombs. I'll ring and see if they still have it. Their auction was today but I don't know whether it reached them in time to enter, or if it did whether it sold. I put a sensible reserve on it.'

'Bloody well better not have sold! Bloody well not!' He banged his umbrella on the floor, causing another shower of drops. His cheeks went from red to white to red again.

I feared he might be about to have a heart attack or stroke. An inconvenience in the shop, although it would at least remove the problem. 'I'll ring them now, Mr Coombs.'

'You do that, Mr Gold!' he bellowed. 'You do that!'

The thirty-something couple opened the door. They were both wearing Barbours and matching hats and they stopped as if Gerald Coombs's shouting had hit them in the face.

I've long suspected there's something missing in me. On the fortunately rare occasions when people get angry, justified or not, I become colder and calmer. Instead of sparking an equal and opposite reaction, which might be more honest and which the situation might merit, their yielding to the atavistic joy of anger makes me curious as to what else must be going on inside them to provoke such a reaction. Of course, I understand the temptation to anger, the pleasure of giving way, telling oneself that one couldn't help it and is therefore not responsible. But I can't share it. The more someone loses control, the more of a sinking iceberg I become, showing less and less of myself. I once caused great offence – purple-faced, apoplectic, table-thumping rage followed by a chair-overturning exit – by simply asking, 'Is that all?' after someone had unburdened himself of a litany of my offences. I had meant it no more than literally, in that if there was anything else, he might as well have said it then, but it obviously came across as insolence. The row was ostensibly about the division of a restaurant bill but of course there was more than that behind it. When he and I met again, years later, we resumed friendly terms as if nothing had happened.

I said nothing more to Gerald Coombs but walked to the phone and rang the auction house, making eye-contact on the way with the thirty-somethings, nodding and smiling and waving them in. They left.

Gerald remained planted in the middle of the shop like a great sulky bear that was unsure what to do next. When I'd finished the call I came around my desk and walked up to him, within striking range had he wished. I was still wondering whether his out-burst was in part a genetic inheritance, remembering that his seventeenth-century ancestor (assuming he was one) William Combe, Thomas's elder brother, was notorious for his splenetic outbursts. 'We're in luck, Mr Coombs. Your desk was in the auction but unsold because it failed to make the reserve I put on it. I'll arrange for it to be recovered and delivered to you. Presumably you won't now be needing the roll-top?'

I half-wished he would take a swipe at me with his umbrella. I wanted him to go too far so that retribution – I had no idea in what form – would be justified. Or at least feel justified.

But he merely stood, blinking behind his glasses, his jowls no longer red with rage. Then he spoke softly, almost absent-mindedly, as if reminded of some minor detail. 'Yes, yes, fine. No, shan't be wanting the roll-top. Kind of you, very kind.' Then he turned and left the shop, leaving only his puddle. I never saw the thirty-something couple again.

Within a couple of days he had his father's desk and the roll-top was back in the shop. I could, of course, have billed him for my costs but, apart from wishing to maintain my reputation for goodwill, I wanted him – them – to feel morally in my debt. It didn't always work like that; some people are blithely unaware of unstated social obligations, while others are aware but selfishly determined to ignore them. Others again quietly exploit them, which I suppose is what I was trying to do.

Anyway, it worked with the Coombses. Some days after the desk-reversal Mrs Coombs rang. She sounded nervous and spoke more rapidly than usual. 'Mr Gold, I'm so sorry we haven't been in today. We intended to but we've been so busy and everything's so – and Gerald has not been well.'

'Oh dear, I'm sorry to hear that.'

'Thank you, that's most kind. It's a chesty thing, he's vulnerable to them but nearly over it now. No, we were wondering – you're quite well, I hope?'

'Yes, thank you, fingers crossed. And you?'

'Oh yes, yes, thank you, I'm always – it's only Gerald who – well, with one thing and another. No, but we were wondering if you were – if you weren't doing anything else but I expect you're terribly busy with the shop and everything and Stephanie. It must be nonstop, isn't it?'

I assured her that things had been pleasantly quiet and under control recently. That meant, of course, that I had sold nothing and was losing money but I doubted that would occur to her.

'Oh good, good, it's so important to rest while you can, isn't it? Yes, yes.' She sounded as if she were agreeing to something else I'd said and was waiting for me to go on. I let her wait. 'And so, yes,' she continued eventually, 'we were – Gerald and I – we were wondering if you'd ... you'd ... be free to come to dinner on Saturday?'

I pretended to consult my diary and said I'd be delighted. She then immediately apologised for the occasion, belittling it in advance – just a few friends, local people, nobody very – but nice people, a kitchen supper really, nothing special, they'd got out of the habit of big dinner parties, she hoped it wouldn't be too boring for me. She seemed unable to bring the conversation to a close until I helped her out by asking after the desk. 'I hope Mr Coombs is happy to have it back, is he?'

'Oh yes, yes, that was so kind of you. I don't know what came over him, he blows hot and cold over these family things. One day he's all for getting rid of everything and the next he's saying how nothing must go, how important it is to preserve things, and then the day after he's complaining about the burden of it all. Makes it almost impossible for anyone to do the right thing. Me included.' She laughed another high tinkling laugh, but she sounded more fluent and confident now. 'I hope he wasn't rude to you? He can be rude. He doesn't mean it.'

'He was clearly very concerned.'

'He gets rather worked up, I'm afraid, overwrought sometimes. But he's very grateful for what you did, getting the old one back. I asked him about the family name, by the way. He said that it did used to be Combe but that it changed around the turn of the nineteenth century, no one knows why. And the swords, yes, they're all family swords.'

'All of them or just the ones on the wall?'

'All, he said, so I suppose he means the poker one as well.'

Chapter Three

During the days and nights before Saturday I barely
ceased thinking or dreaming about the sword.
Frustratingly, my memory of it became fuzzier the
more I tried to recall detail: was the blade really triangular in cross-section with a single hollow-ground
ridge or were there two ridges which would make
it squared? How long was it, what pattern was the
guard, did it look like a fashionable French, Italian or
Spanish design or was it a plainer Germanic or English
piece and, if the latter, what was the difference? I determined to find out more about swords before Saturday,
though I doubted I would get much time to examine it.

It wasn't only the sword itself that occupied – I
almost said obsessed – me. I also thought constantly of
its original owner. If I was right that he got it with his
coat of arms, did he buy it off the shelf or have it made,
and if so by whom and where? How much would that

have cost? Or might he already have owned it? After all, swords were commonly used by actors in stage fights – there are stage directions for fights or duels in over a dozen of his plays and they were popular with audiences, many of whom might have been similarly armed themselves. It was not unknown for there to be spontaneous audience participation in stage fights. Acting troupes would have owned swords and some actors were well known as good swordsmen – one of the great comedians, Richard Tarleton, was a Master of Fencing. Shakespeare is said to have learned to fence at the Blackfriars theatre, to which his business partner and leading actor, Richard Burbage, had annexed a fencing school, in which Shakespeare was also part-ner. Academics, I read, had counted 437 references to swords in the Shakespearian canon, and five to duels.

It is thus perfectly possible that Shakespeare acquired his sword from the company he part-owned. But I suspect he would have wanted something special to signify his new status and would have been prepared to pay for it. Rapiers in particular were not cheap – in *Hamlet* the King wagers six Barbary horses against six French rapiers and *poignards*, with girdles and hangers and so on. The kind of sword you wore was as much a mark of status as of your willingness and ability to defend yourself.

The prospect of having to defend your life or your purse was far from remote among the theatres, stews, bear-pits, cockpits and brothels of the South Bank, beyond the authority of the City of London. My researches among the fractious acting community revealed that the actor Gabriel Spencer, whom Ben Jonson was to kill two years later, killed James Feake in a fight in 1596, while the playwright John Day killed another, Henry Porter, with a rapier. Shakespeare would have known these men. Indeed, William Knell, an actor with the Queen's Men, was killed in a fight in Stratford in 1587 shortly before the troupe was due to perform. Shakespeare, if he were there, must have known about that, too, as he would of many other instances when swords were drawn without fatal consequences. Thus, he might well have carried a sword for self-protection even before acquiring his gentlemanly status. It seems that the 1573 proclamation banning the wearing of swords, daggers and spurs by any who were not 'knights and baron's sons, and others of high degree and place' was widely ignored in a city in which most men carried knives.

But, unlike some of his more violence-prone colleagues, Shakespeare himself seems not to have been involved in fights, duels or any other kind of fracas apart from one curious incident in a snowstorm on 28 December 1598. This occurred when he and others of his troupe, the then Chamberlain's Men, went in the evening armed with 'swords, daggers, bills, axes and such like' to dismantle their playhouse, the Theatre, and transport its timbers across the river to build what became the Globe. The landlord of the Theatre was away for Christmas and friends of his tried to stop them, vainly, though there appears to have been no violence. Subsequent legal proceedings, initiated by the landlord – he owned the land but not the building – came to nothing.

I tried to imagine daily life with a sword. Would he have troubled with it every time he left his lodgings, donning girdle and hanger before crossing the river to Bankside by ferry (which would have cost him) or by the crowded London Bridge? It would surely have been a significant encumbrance to any man going about his daily business, not least because the blades then were so long – like Gerald's – that the weapon, stood on its point, was supposed to reach its owner's shoulder. Would he have taken it off when he sat down to write? In fact, where did he write – in his lodgings before leaving for the playhouse or by candlelight when he returned? Easier and cheaper to write in daylight. Whenever he did it, he did it fast – thirty-seven plays plus sonnets and poems, as well as we know not what else. And all the time rehearsing, acting and managing. And if he didn't carry his sword with him, where could he have kept it securely?

Then there were his journeys out of London. John Aubrey, seventeenth-century antiquarian and marvellous recorder of gossip, wrote that Shakespeare 'was wont to go into Warwickshire once a year' but modern scholars think it was probably more often. His direct route, via Beaconsfield, High Wycombe, Stokenchurch, Oxford, Woodstock, Enstone and Chipping Norton, was about ninety-four miles. That meant a good three to five days' ride, depending on weather and road conditions, through a busy agricultural landscape populated by vagrants, sturdy beggars and discharged soldiers and sailors. Sensible, perhaps, to travel armed if you could. I read how that other literary colossus, Geoffrey Chaucer, was mugged – as we would now call it – in 1390 when carrying wages from central London to Eltham Palace in Kent, in his role as Clerk of the King's Works.

I also read a story about Shakespeare's sojourns at the Crown in Oxford where he was godfather to the host's son, young William Davenant, future poet and playwright. The story is that his relations with Mrs Davenant were rumoured in the town to be such that the 'god' in 'godfather' was redundant. One who might have known the truth of this, as well as about the sword and other incidentals of Shakespeare's life, was William Greenaway, Stratford's main carter or carrier. His family were neighbours of the Shakespeares in Henley Street and he frequently travelled to and from London with goods, mail, messages and news. When Shakespeare journeyed back to Stratford he probably paid five shillings to hire a horse from Greenaway at the Bell Inn, near St Paul's. They might have travelled together via either Oxford or Banbury, given that there was safety in numbers and that Greenaway would have known the routes and places to stay better than anyone. In jogging companionably together, William Greenaway could have heard more of the daily details of Shakespeare's life than almost anyone else – certainly he'd have known whether he travelled armed – but not a word survives.

I spent time, too, researching Gerald Coombs's family, at least as far as I could online. Much of it merely reinforced what I knew already: that Combe was not an uncommon name and that without further research it was impossible to confirm whether Thomas Combe and Gerald Coombs were of the same stock. I could follow Thomas's family down to near the end of the seventeenth century and Gerald's back into the late eighteenth but for the intervening century or so I would need to spend time in the National Archives and among parish and graveyard registers. Time, however, was what I felt I did not have; anyway, I knew enough to be sure, or thought I did. The Warwickshire connection and that seventeenth-century portrait of William Combe were sufficient, if not conclusive.

Meanwhile, I plotted. I would have that sword. What I would do with it, I hadn't decided. The trick was to establish that it was plausibly Shakespeare's without alerting Gerald Coombs to its value. What would he do if he knew? Probably he'd simply hang on to it. He didn't seem to need money and didn't appear to be strongly financially motivated. Certainly, he wouldn't like to feel he was being ripped off – that was clear from our conversation about the desk – but the fact of possession would probably mean more to him than the prospect of reward. Most of my best customers were like that, though I suspected he differed from them in one respect: he would keep the sword not so much because he valued it, or because he worshipped Shakespeare or was in any way excited or moved by his plays, but through inertia and indifference, and because it was his. I had detected in him no spark of interest in literature or the arts, nor even a wish to feign it in order to seem informed or to keep up with fashion. Probably his friends were like that too, if he had any. I wasn't sure how Mrs Coombs would react but Gerald, I was convinced, would do no more than grunt at the news that he owned Shakespeare's sword and go on using it as a poker. Or, in a fit of exasperation at any intrusion arising from the discovery, would throw it into the canal at the foot of the rock on which Winchelsea is built. He didn't deserve it, I told myself.

That was how I felt then. Already, he and even Mrs Coombs were mere adjuncts to the sword in my mind. I liked her for her apparent diffidence and gentleness of manner, while her looks reminded me of Philip Larkin's line to the effect that 'a face, in those days, was enough to start the whole shooting match off'. Perhaps not quite a shooting match at my age but those misty blue eyes and vulnerable expression were enough to provoke an uplifting rattle of musketry. Also, I felt sorry for a woman so obviously bullied and put upon by her boorish husband. But the sword was the thing.

During my first and younger bachelorhood I enjoyed dinner parties, not least as an opportunity for mate-hunting (though I can't now recall that any significant relationships emerged). Later, as one half of a married couple, the shine gradually wore off and they became wearisomely competitive, an obligatory social ritual for parading as a social unit. Then, when children came along – though not for Amanda and me – they were dominated by middle-class baby talk and school talk, which become even more competitive.

Invitations declined after divorce, then picked up a little when I became useful for gender balance. For a while I was even a prospect for remarriage, until age eased me into that obscure corner of the market that no one looks into until they get there. Surprisingly, in my second bachelorhood, my enjoyment of dinner parties returned. No longer hunting, no longer competing, I took pleasure in an evening out, in being fed and watered and in having amiable, undemanding conversations with people as boring and grateful as myself. It made a change from dining at home with Stephanie who – a hangover from her institutional years – eats contentedly only in front of the television.

Mrs Coombs answered the door wearing a simple pale-blue dress and a sapphire and diamond necklace. I was the first to arrive and my proffered bunch of flowers threw her into consternation as she struggled to express delight and gratitude while finding somewhere to put them and greeting the next guests whose car had just drawn up. After some seconds of fun and fluster I took them from her and cleared a space on the crowded kitchen table, returning to the hall in time to relieve her of an almost identical bunch brought by the next guests. I briefly considered a search for vases but the kitchen was cluttered with crockery, pots, pans, bottles, cooking implements and dainty bowls of chilled green soup that looked unfortunately like urological samples. I gave up and left them on the windowsill. More guests had meanwhile arrived and were being ushered into the drawing room. There was no sign of Gerald Coombs.

One of the banes of middle-class life is that we have inherited from our forebears the assumption that entertaining means three or four courses plus wine, spirits and tea or coffee. It can work but all too often the evening proceeds with the lumbering stateliness of an overladen Spanish galleon, while most of us – already overweight and overfed – would prefer a nimble English frigate of a repast. But no one dares say so and, when it comes to their turn to host, none has the nerve to limit provision to that which nearly all secretly want. We do as we have been done by, condemning ourselves to long processional evenings in perpetuity.

At the same time, it is impossible for most hosts – hostesses especially – to relax and enjoy it. They may bask in the afterglow of everything having gone well, boosted by exaggerated thank-you letters, but at the time and for days before they will have been riven with all the anxiety and tension of a theatrical performance. Added to which, they have to do it all themselves, with no stagehands, scene-shifters, ushers or lighting operators. Their forebears had cooks and servants to sustain these elaborate performances but nowadays the hostess, exhausted before it starts, feels she has to serve and supervise everyone while paying full attention to each guest. This makes it impossible to have a satisfactory conversation with the poor woman because her eyes and mind are on whose glass needs filling, who is merely picking at the food, who hasn't had the gravy, who is being ignored by the men on either side of her and by her own husband's flirtation with the actress wife of the drunken lawyer at the end of the table. Not to mention the state of the pudding in the oven.

Charlotte coped better than most. Although obviously anxious, she had – has – an unobtrusive organisational ability that meant that everything worked. She also deployed her happy knack of getting others to speak about themselves while appearing to listen and saying little herself, so that she could keep an eye on everyone else. She did this without help from Gerald, who appeared only when all the guests had arrived and she had seen to their drinks. He was upstairs, would be down soon, she said when I offered to help. He appeared wearing blazer and golf club tie, unhurried and unsmiling. Only one of the other men wore a tie, a retired judge.

I set myself up as the model guest that night, fetching and carrying, refilling glasses, facilitating conversation, engaging the neglected. In other words, doing everything a hostess might normally expect her husband to do. Gerald took no notice, talking most of the time across the table to the retired judge who, it soon became all too apparent, was another keen golfer. His plump wife, desperate not to be ignored, was happy to talk to anyone about anything, so I paid her special attention. She was well informed about the history of Winchelsea, particularly its late-nineteenth-century difficulties with drainage.

The other couple were farmers from the Romney Marsh, pleasant inoffensive people who gave the impression that they were pleased, if somewhat surprised, to find themselves there. It turned out they knew the Coombses because the wife and Charlotte had sat on the local hospice committee together. The Marsh is famously productive farmland and, since they seemed to own a lot of it, I assumed they were wealthy. 'Windmills,' I heard the husband say when asked what was the most profitable crop these days.

The other guest was Eileen, whose gender-balance I assumed I was. A doctor in general practice, she wore no make-up and kept her iron-grey hair tied tightly in a bun. Her plain grey trouser-suit looked like a uniform and she soon made sure we all knew she had been on call that day. She seemed ready to be irritated from the moment she crossed the threshold and it was impossible not to suspect that this was a chronic condition. Before we sat at table she had lectured the farming couple on the overuse of chemicals.

It pleased me that she was so aggressively unappealing. I dislike doctors and anyone else who lives by telling us what is good for us. In earlier times I would have hated the clergy but I tolerate them now that their functions have been secularised and they no longer matter. However, I was also pleased with Eileen because she so obviously set out to be unpleasing that I could take her as evidence that people really had given up trying to pair me off. Not that I would object to being paired off, occasionally and briefly, with appealing women who were similarly inclined, but I had no wish to remarry or embroil myself in any form of permanent intimacy. Marriage – at least, in my recollection – is a matter of perpetual manoeuvring and I had lost my appetite for the inconveniences entailed.

The idea of online dating, occasionally suggested, filled me with horror.

Having taken against Eileen on sight, therefore, I also took a perverse pleasure in making myself agreeable to her. She had been a neighbour of the Coombses before moving to Hastings following the break-up of her marriage to another doctor. I joined her in extolling the illusory delights of Hastings, a depressing mess of a town that for decades has supposedly been up-and-coming but never quite does; or, if it does, gets there only after everywhere else has been up and gone. We agreed that living in poorer areas was more 'real' than living in posh, rarefied Winchelsea, though it then came out that she lived in the newly gentrified Hastings Old Town. I relish such middle-class snobbery, with its assumption that virtue is the prerogative of the (relatively) poor. Sometimes, by seeming to agree, it's possible to get people close to insisting that the poor are morally superior simply because they are poor. Most shy away at the last jump, but they don't abandon their assumptions. With Eileen I more or less succeeded.

'You feel closer to the essentials of life, living where you now do?' I asked.

She shook her head. 'The essentials don't change, of course, they're the same for everyone. But if you mean, do I feel that the people I live among are less cushioned and blinkered by wealth and possessions, therefore more aware of deprivation and what it does to people and therefore more likely to sympathise, then, yes, I feel closer to them.'

'You find them morally more sympathetic?'

'Morally more aware, certainly.' She spoke now with a certain wariness, uneasy perhaps at finding herself in agreement with someone who was neither a caring professional nor one of the virtuous poor. Indeed, a man in trade, an antiques dealer, at that; probably on a par with estate agents.

'More deserving themselves, perhaps? In that they're less culpable and less blinded to the sufferings of others?'

'More deserving, yes.'

I nodded sympathetically, forbearing to describe Stephanie's and my early childhood in a north Kent council estate where enthusiasm for the material things of life and devil take the hindmost left little room for the self-regarding comforts of altruism.

I broke off to help Charlotte – as I was now asked to call her – clear away the main course. Gerald and the retired judge didn't notice, oblivious of hands removing their plates and of the chorus of compliments on the now-departed sea bass.

In the kitchen Charlotte cleared a space for my stack of dinner plates. 'You're being naughty, aren't you, Simon?'

'Just trying to be helpful.'

'With Eileen, I mean. You're not as nice as you seem,

are you? You're teasing her.' She smiled. 'Don't worry, I'm rather relieved you're not perfect.'

'Just seeing how far she would go in that direction. I don't think she sees I'm teasing.'

'I'm sure she doesn't. Nothing if not literal-minded, Eileen.'

She clearly saw through me, which meant there was no point in trying to excuse myself, but I couldn't help trying. 'It's just that I think the rich are what the poor would be if they had money and the poor behave just as the rich would if they didn't.'

She wasn't interested. 'If you could get those trays we'll take one each.'

We loaded the plates and made for the door together, which forced us to pause facing each other, our laden trays between us. 'You have such beautiful eyes,' I said, not because she does – though she does – but because it seemed a good time to say it and I wanted to impress her. I also felt an obscure urge to surprise her, as if that would gain me some advantage.

She smiled at me almost pityingly, shook her head and moved on.

The rest of the evening was helped by the fact that we had a little of that rare, ever-to-be-desired thing, a general conversation in which everyone joined. It concerned a local perennial, the ever-threatened, never-enacted bypass. The problem is that there is no room to seaward without disfiguring the coastline and no room inland without despoiling beautiful valleys. Eileen couldn't see what was wrong with a fourteen-mile tunnel, although she disapproved of anything that encouraged more traffic to damage the environment. The farmer's wife thought existing roads should be left unrepaired to discourage through traffic, the judge foresaw entire careers in litigation during the appeals process, Gerald grunted and said it would never happen. I agreed with everyone while pondering what Charlotte had meant by saying she was relieved that I wasn't as nice as I seemed. It was true, of course, and her recognition of it suggested it applied equally to her; it takes one to know one. But I had yet to see whatever was not nice in her.

I helped with the teas and coffees. Gerald and the judge wanted brandies. As I placed Gerald's before him he acknowledged me for the first time that evening. 'Good of you –er – very good, very good.' He had clearly forgotten my name.

As the now tacitly acknowledged unpaid home help, I remained to clear up after the others left. Charlotte tried not very hard to urge me to go, saying I must be exhausted after a week in the shop and that my poor sister must be anxious. But I was determined to stay since there had been no chance either to talk to Gerald about his family or to examine the sword again. Throughout the evening, between every sentence and every mouthful, the thought of it lying in the hearth waiting to be touched, held, sensed, was like the prospect of secret sex.

Gerald disappeared upstairs while Charlotte and I cleared up, reappearing only when we were almost done. He stood motionless by the kitchen table like a great ship moored in harbour while lesser craft plied around it, making no attempt to clear or carry, fill the dishwasher or put things away. Nor did he join our broken conversation as we dodged around him. He seemed completely unaware of us. Eventually, when I was drying some of the things that Charlotte had washed because they wouldn't fit in the dishwasher, he said, 'Need two really.'

I looked at him. 'Two?'

'Dishwashers. Then you'd have room for everything. Things could go from dishwasher to table to the other dishwasher. More efficient, less shelf space needed.'

I wondered if he was drunk. It was hard to say because, now I thought about it, he usually looked or sounded half-drunk. But what he'd just said made sense. Two dishwashers would indeed be handy.

He turned to face me. 'Grateful for your help.'

'More than grateful,' said Charlotte, stepping round him to wipe the table and giggling again.

'Nightcap?' asked Gerald. 'One for the road? Not supposed to say that now, of course, but you know what I mean.'

'Do, please, we've almost finished,' said Charlotte.

I hung the damp tea towel on the Aga rail and followed Gerald back into the drawing room. I'd drunk little over dinner and so joined him with a malt whisky. While he poured I again surveyed his ancestors, reckoning there was no harm in showing interest nor in lingering by the seventeenth-century one. With his long hair and plain brown jacket he could easily have been a preacher. If it had been more than head and shoulders it might have shown him carrying something – a bible, perhaps, or even a sword. Charlotte had shown me that it was entitled 'William Combe' but a date would be helpful, especially if it fitted with cousin William to whom Thomas left the bulk of his estate.

Gerald joined me in front of the portrait, holding the whiskies. 'Miserable old sod.'

Coming from you, that's something, I thought, searching the two faces for resemblances. Apart from a shared lack of any desire to please, there was nothing. William's long grey hair was abundant, his lips were thin and his grey-blue eyes looked out with an earnest, unyielding stare. Gerald had fuller, coarser features, much less hair and passive brown eyes conveying nothing of William's determination.

'I'm trying to see if it's dated,' I said, peering. 'You don't happen to know?'

'Could be something on the back.'

'May I?' I put down my whisky, removed the painting and took it over to the standard lamp. The back was blank paper browned with age, the black frame was heavy and certainly old, possibly original. His name was written in small black capitals in the bottom-right corner of the painting but I couldn't tell whether it was contemporary or a later addition. There was lettering squeezed beneath it, smaller and less distinct. The first word looked like 'of' and the second, much longer, began with an 'A' but was impossible to decipher thereafter. It was long enough to be Alvechurch, the Worcestershire village where William Combe lived, roughly twenty miles from Stratford and now just south of the M42. There was no sign of the name or initials of the painter. A professional clean and modern dating techniques could doubtless tell us more. I said so to Gerald.

He shook his head. 'No point.'

'You wouldn't like to know more about it? Or about the sitter, your ancestor?'

'Dead. All dead, aren't they? No point.'

He turned away and stood facing the hearth, staring into the empty grate. I rehung the painting and joined him. The fire irons, including the sword, were neatly arranged. 'I could clean that up for you, too. I could do that myself.'

'What – the fireplace?'

'No, the sword. That one, the one you use as a poker.'

He stared as if he had never noticed it before. 'What d'you want to do that for? No point.'

'It might clean up well. It might turn out to be valuable.' I didn't want to convince him of that but it was worth the risk if I could persuade him to let me take it away.

'Nothing special. Can't be. Not like those.' He nodded at the swords on the wall. 'Used in action, those. Probably. Good condition, too. Not like that old thing.'

I suffered another spasm of temptation, the insane moral impulse to confess, to tell him whose sword I thought it was, to urge him to cherish it or sell it for a great deal of money. But I controlled myself. 'Did your father ever say anything about it?'

'Kept it here, where it is. Always been a poker, long as I can remember.'

I didn't want to show too keen an interest, so I said, 'Another thing, your long-case clock on the landing, the local clock, the one by H. Bourn of Rye. Charlotte showed me it.'

'In the family since new, I believe. They knew the maker.'

'She said you'd stopped it because the chime kept you awake. But it's easy to disconnect the chime, the work of a few minutes. I could pop up and do it sometime.' That would be another excuse to visit.

For once his eyes showed some interest. 'Could you, could you now? Very kind.' He stared again into the empty grate. 'Very kind,' he whispered.

Again, it was unclear whether the conversation had ended. I longed to pick up the sword and, to stop myself, added, 'I'll arrange to call in and do it sometime.'

There was no reaction. I would have yielded to temptation and picked up the sword after a few more seconds if he hadn't then said, 'Charlotte – she, you know – doesn't get out much. I – I'm not much good for – if you come across anything locally that she'd like, you know, talks, plays, concerts and things ...'

'I'll certainly let you know.'

'... Happy for you to take her if you'd – you know – if I'm busy with something.'

He trailed off, still staring into the fireplace. As well as not being sure he'd finished, I wasn't sure what he meant. Did he mean exactly and only what he said or was he offering me Charlotte? If so, with or without her cognisance? It was hard to imagine him ever being busy. I had started saying something to the effect that I was pleased and honoured when she came in from the kitchen.

'Oh good,' she said. 'I'm glad you're enjoying your nightcaps. One always needs to unwind after these things.'

Gerald ignored her, fixated, it seemed, on the fireplace. I felt confident enough now to step into his shoes – or, rather, his deep-red leather slippers. 'And how about you? Can I get you something?'

She smiled as at a child who is doing well but needs

encouragement. 'So sweet of you but not this time, thank you.' She tinkled again.

We made conversation, awkwardly because of the pretence of including Gerald, who ignored us both. I asked about the other guests and made exaggeratedly complimentary remarks about them, mentioning Eileen in particular as lively and stimulating. Charlotte smiled at that. Eventually, when I said it was time I went and Charlotte had made the ritual protests, Gerald responded by turning away from the fireplace and accompanying us into the hall. As Charlotte opened the front door and I was about to shake his hand, he said, 'He . . . he always said – my father – said it was given to the family by Shakespeare. You know, William Shakespeare, chap who wrote those plays. The sword, I mean.'

'Really? How fascinating. Did he have any evidence or was it just family lore?'

'No knowing the truth of it, of course. He also said a violin we have is a Stradivari which it is not. My uncle had a chap look at it. It's a copy. It's in the cellar.'

'But the sword? You never—?'

'Always used it as a poker. He wouldn't have done that if he really thought there was something in it.'

'I could get an expert to—'

Gerald turned away, half-raising his hand. 'Goodnight. Come again.'

Chapter Four

A couple of weeks later I discovered that on the Tuesday following there was a local historical society talk on the Roman settlement in our part of Sussex. I was not a member but promptly joined via the website, intending to ring Charlotte and invite her – assuming, that is, that she knew of her husband's suggestion. But over dinner on the Sunday before, when Stephanie and I always had roast chicken, which I had taught Stephanie to do and which gave her a reliable weekly pleasure, she suddenly said, 'She rang. On the telephone. The lady.'

I guessed whom she meant. 'When was that?'

She paused with full fork half raised and a dribble of gravy running down her chin. 'Before.'

To Stephanie, the past is indivisible. 'Was it a long time ago or was it today, before you started cooking?'

'Today, when you were out. She rang.'

'What did she say?'

Stephanie laughed. She has a rich, infectious laugh, throaty and unselfconscious. More gravy dribbled. 'She said a lot!'

I smiled encouragingly. 'I expect she did. Can you remember what it was?'

Her laugh mutated into coughing and hiccoughing. Eventually, when she had herself more or less back under control, she said, 'She said please will you ring her.' She was convulsed by another paroxysm of merriment, tears running unheeded down her cheeks. 'She said you are a good waiter!'

It transpired that Charlotte had rung to suggest the very talk I had spotted. 'I wouldn't dream of pushing myself on you,' she said when I rang, 'only Gerald said you had very kindly offered to accompany me to local cultural functions which he hasn't time to go to – in his words.' She laughed. 'And so when I saw this one, I thought, seize the moment. If you're free, that is. And only if you're interested in the Romans. Not everyone is, of course.'

It was soon settled. I told her I had been about to make the same suggestion but I'm not sure she believed me. Her version of how the arrangement came about did nothing to dispel the mystery of Gerald's motive, or hers.

'I had a lovely long chat with Stephanie,' she added. 'She was very amused when I told her what a wonderful guest you were, all that waitering and serving.'

'She told me. She's still laughing about it. It was very kind of you to talk to her. People don't usually make the effort. They're too embarrassed.'

'Well, you have to give her time, no good being in a hurry, but she's wonderfully straightforward. Comes straight out with it.'

I continued my researches into the Combe family. Successive wills made no mention of the sword. Gerald's father's assertion was encouraging, of course, but it hardly constituted evidence and so was really no more than tantalising. Perhaps there was evidence somewhere, perhaps Gerald, given time – like Stephanie – might one day say, offhandedly, 'Yes, there's a letter about it somewhere. In the loft.' Or the cellar he had mentioned. Winchelsea houses are known for their cavernous cellars hewn from rock. In the summer months they hold open days on which the curious are led up and down flights of narrow stone steps. The function of the cellars was not, as popularly supposed, to conceal contraband but legitimately to store the wines and spirits and other goods in which the ancient port traded.

Clearly, I had to get into their cellar. Who knew what might be there, fake Stradivari apart. Most cellars are damp, dank places but the few Winchelsea ones I had been in were dry and cool, ideal for storage. Perhaps I would discover some cloak or costume in faded red cloth. I had just read that when the old queen died at last in 1603 things were not looking good for Shakespeare and his company of players, the Chamberlain's Men. The Lord Chamberlain was their patron at court but he also died, leaving them without commissions or protection. But in May 1603 the new king, James, unexpectedly authorised Shakespeare and his eight fellow shareholders to call themselves the King's Men, performing at court, at the Globe and throughout the realm. They were given official court status as Grooms of the Chamber, which was when they were each issued with four and a half yards of red cloth to be fashioned into royal livery for state occasions. He would surely have worn his sword then. The Coombses' cellar could be an Aladdin's cave.

I also researched Gerald himself, expecting a lucrative professional or City background from which he had retired early on a comfortable pension. Stockbroking, perhaps, or Lloyd's; or maybe he had owned and built up a business which he had then sold, though it was hard to imagine the Gerald I knew doing anything energetically. But it was none of these, in fact nothing very much of anything. He had attended a boarding school in Sussex, had not gone to university – not many people did then – had worked in some undisclosed role for a freight transport company, then was marketing manager of a foodstuffs company, was briefly manager of a chain of furniture stores, then head of sales and marketing for an engineering firm which went into liquidation, following which he was involved with two banks and an insurance company. His final recorded position was again in marketing, this time with a rail company that lost its franchise. He had stayed nowhere long, seemed never to have achieved distinction in anything and had retired early, but obviously not uncomfortably. Presumably family money helped. I would have to find out more about his father. Charlotte, whose maiden name I had yet to discover, did not appear to have done anything of public record.

The Roman talk was in Battle, an inland town a comfortable half-hour drive away. That, I thought, would give more time to relax her and condition her to my purpose. Gerald did not appreciate the sword, had no interest in it, felt no responsibility for it and so did not deserve it. What I would do with it and precisely how I would get it, I hadn't decided, but I was sure that the getting of it would have to involve Charlotte. I felt I was flowing with the tide but had yet to identify a precise landfall. Like a mariner of old, I imagined, I would know it when I saw it and, seeing it, would know the means.

'Are you always so punctual?' She answered the door herself, wearing black slacks and a smart, high-shouldered jacket. She closed the door without calling goodbye to Gerald.

It was a pleasant early-evening drive along a ridge between two valleys, then winding through woods until not far from the historic town. We tried to discuss things Roman, professing enthusiasm and ignorance in equal measure. I noticed her end-of-sentence giggle more that evening, though whether because she was doing it more or because I was waiting for it, I couldn't say. I wondered how long I should have to be in her company before I found it a serious irritant. Possibly I had such mannerisms too, but, being unaware of them, I couldn't imagine anyone taking significant objection.

The talk, by the county archaeologist, was practised and informative. I couldn't now repeat a word of it except his answer to a question about the Roman short sword. This was partly because my thoughts circled constantly around that hearth back in Winchelsea and partly because I was considering whether Charlotte was aware of our thighs touching. We were all crowded on narrow, uncomfortable, village hall-type chairs and I became aware that we were touching very soon after the talk started. I couldn't decide whether it was deliberate on her part or accidental and, if the latter, whether she was aware and, if so, why she hadn't moved. I could have moved away, of course, but she might have interpreted that as rejection, which was not the message I wanted to send. At the same time, although I found her desirable, I hesitated to embark on an affair since that could cut either way when it came to securing the sword. One the one hand, she might help me to it; on the other, if she suspected that the sword was my real passion it would have the opposite effect. The touch was anyway so slight it was possible she was genuinely unaware. I did not move.

The talk excited her. I could see it in her eyes when she turned to me during the applause. I suspected it wasn't so much the subject – interesting enough but not often a cause of arousal – as the occasion. Being part of an informed audience which asked good questions engendered in her a social and intellectual excitement. She turned to me, clapping and smiling as if I had given the talk myself.

There was wine afterwards. Since neither of us knew anyone there we could talk uninterrupted. 'Fascinating,' she said. 'So many people who know so much. Makes me feel so ignorant.'

The faces around us were middle-aged and upward, mostly retired professionals. My kind of customer. I decided then and there to attend regularly, get to know people, maybe work my way onto the committee. They clustered thickly round the speaker, who had offered to take further questions over wine. Partly with my new ambition in mind, and partly through genuine curiosity, I asked Charlotte if she minded if we lingered long enough for me to ask a question.

'Ask any number,' she said. 'It's all so interesting.'

My question, when I'd forged a path through the

throng, was about the Roman short sword: why was it the length it was and why were later swords longer? It was a genuine question, in that I was mildly curious, but of course my main reason for asking was precautionary: to establish in Charlotte's eyes that I had an interest in swords in general as cover for my interest in the poker. Disclaiming any serious knowledge of swords, our speaker nonetheless had a pretty good stab at the answer. It was partly that the technology of making iron then meant that they could make short blades that were reliably strong but longer blades were prone to break. Also, Roman soldiers were trained to fight in close formation, sword in one hand, shield in the other. The shield was held so as to protect their front and left side, while with their sword they were supposed to take on the enemy to their right, who would be engaging their comrade on the right. This, and the shortness of their two-edged blades – less than two feet – made killing a physically intimate business. That was a remark I was to recall later.

We talked most of the way home about the ubiquity of the Romans in our part of the world, their ports and garrisons and local evidence of the scale of their iron industry. She was stimulated to find out more, she said, it was almost criminal to live among so much history and ignore it. Then, as I slowed to enter Winchelsea through one of the medieval gateways, she said, 'When we first met, when Gerald and I came into your shop that day, I asked if you were an obsessive. A bit cheeky, I know but I thought you wouldn't mind.' She tinkled. 'And you denied it.'

'I did, yes. I seem to remember the accusation was because of what I was saying about the **Sèvres** porcelain. I said I was a magpie.'

'It wasn't an accusation, there's nothing wrong with being an obsessive. But I think you were wrong to deny it. You are one. You're obsessive about swords.'

'What – because I asked that question?'

'Not only that. I watched you when you were looking at our swords, especially the poker one. It intrigues you, doesn't it, that one? I could tell.'

I'd no idea she'd noticed. My ploy hadn't worked. If anything, it had had the opposite effect and drawn attention to my desire. I felt as if I'd been caught doing something illicit or, worse, a squalid breach of decorum. Essentially, of course, I was guilty of both, except that I hadn't actually done anything, not yet. 'The essence of a lie is the intent to deceive,' my father once said, a remark that struck home like an arrow. I didn't often lie outright but I lied now to Charlotte by admitting only to curiosity. 'Oh, that old rapier with the swept hilt? Yes, it does interest me a bit. I think it's quite old, older than the Civil War mortuary sword that's one of those above the fireplace. I was trying to make up my mind whether it's English, French, Spanish, Italian or whatever. The blade is probably German.'

'Gerald told you that story about it being Shakespeare's?'

I pretended that detail had slipped my mind. 'It – oh, yes, yes, you're right, he mentioned that. But he didn't say how or why his father—'

'The Coombses are full of old family stories, most of them nonsense like the Stradivari one. There's probably a family legend about every single thing in our cellar. You must come and have a look one day. It's crammed with old junk.'

We arrived at her garden gate. The back lanes of Winchelsea are almost supernaturally quiet at night and the only sign of life that evening was a disappearing cat. She neither invited me in nor offered the conventional brushing of cheeks but got out promptly, gushing thanks. I hadn't anticipated a demonstrative parting, still less going in, but the clear refusal of either made me feel as if I had and was being denied. I drove home as frustrated and disappointed as in failed youthful courtships. It was as if she had used my interest in the sword to skewer me with it.

I dithered for few days over whether to take her up on her offer to view the cellar. I even considered being honest and simply saying I wanted to examine the sword again. Given what she'd said, there was nothing now to be gained by concealing my interest, so long as I didn't alarm her by revealing the extent of it. But I pondered rather than acted. Doesn't Hamlet go on about how the pale cast of thought inhibits action? I felt I was wandering in a great fog of thought, directionless because my ultimate intention was still unresolved. How far was I prepared to go to get that sword and, having got it, what would I do with it? I certainly didn't think I would kill for it.

Fortunately, business picked up a bit during those few days so there wasn't too much time for pallid musings. A very nice Georgian dining table and chairs flew out of the shop along with a restored Victorian couch and several lamps and other small items. Then one afternoon Charlotte appeared, with the sword.

She had wrapped it in a travelling rug or blanket, the sort people used to have in cars before cars routinely had heaters. I didn't realise what it was at first as we stood talking about the unendingly grey weather. She spoke at a breathless gabble, leaving me worrying about what to say next because any subject was likely to be exhausted within seconds. I hadn't yet learned that she was comfortable with silences, and indeed was adept at exploiting them.

'How is Gerald?' I asked.

'He's away, golfing thing in Norfolk. He's not – not awfully well, probably shouldn't have gone but he's with others so I let him go.' She laughed.

'Golfing widows not allowed?'

'On the contrary, spouses encouraged. It's supposed to be a treat for them. Some of the other wives are going but I' – she laughed again as she unrolled the blanket – 'I brought you this. Thought you might like to examine it properly while Gerald's away. So long as you bring it back before he returns the day after tomorrow. You've seen how it can set him off when things leave the house, even temporarily.'

She held the sword by the hilt, gingerly as if fearing contamination, the point almost on the floor. Stephanie, who was polishing the brass hinges and locks on a Victorian trunk in the window, stared open-mouthed, cloth in hand.

I took the sword. 'That's more than kind of you. I'll be most careful with it and I'll certainly get it back to you in time, I promise.' I held it horizontally in both hands, like a baby presented for christening. 'It'll be difficult – I'll examine it as closely as I can but without cleaning it I'm not sure I'll be able to tell you much about it. I assume if I were to clean it Gerald would notice?'

'Don't worry about that. I'll say I asked our daily to clean it, or say I did it myself. He knows I have cleaning fits now and again.'

'He won't mind?'

'Ring me when you're ready to bring it back. Make sure I'm in.'

'It really is very kind.'

She turned for the door as if suddenly realising what the time was, though she hadn't looked at her watch.

'I must go, I'm sorry, I've got to meet someone. Thank you, thank you so much.'

It was unconvincing, not least because she had made it sound as if I were doing her a favour. I laid the sword reverentially on my desk.

Stephanie stared after her as she crossed the street towards Church Square. She looked back at me, beaming. 'Nice lady.'

'Isn't she? Very kind.'

'Will she come again?'

'I'm sure she will.'

She laughed loudly. 'I hope she does.'

I worked on the sword with cleaning fluids all evening, beginning with the blade and taking care not to use anything that would discolour or corrode. Some of the years – decades, centuries? – of ash and smoke-blackening came off relatively easily but in places the heat seemed to have burned into the metal. I could have done more but didn't want to risk damaging any marks or engravings. Also, if Charlotte had notionally cleaned it herself, it wouldn't do to have it gleaming as if industrial cleaners had been at work. Many of the blades I had seen at the Wallace Collection were far from gleaming, often pock-marked or speckled with age.

But cleaning revealed nothing of its ownership. I had no serious hopes of finding Shakespeare's coat of arms, initials or name; although technically feasible, that was not customary. A maker's mark was much more likely but there was nothing until rubbing revealed 'ME FECIT SOLINGEN'. A German blade, then, as so many were in the years before the swordsmiths of Hounslow came on stream. Solingen was where the best blades in the world were made, then and for centuries to come. It was so famous that other makers would fraudulently imitate its marks but I wasn't expert enough to tell whether this was genuine. It was no surprise that the edges and the point were blunt. Restoring it to its pristine sharpness would demand machinery I didn't have and anyway it would be an unlikely thing for Charlotte to have done. It was best left as it was. I was saying that to myself even as I began gently to file it, surprised at how easily an almost respectable edge and point emerged. It was indeed a quality item.

Individuality was more likely to be found on the hilt. Blades demanded craftsmanship but they could be, and often were, replaced. The hilt, on the other hand, was an exhibition of artistry and the most obvious indication of the wearer's status. The knuckle guard was dented and I discovered that the cross-guard or quillon was missing the bent swan's neck on its lower end; the metal felt rough to my fingertip where it had broken off. Detailing was impossible to see under the blackening and soot but I could feel it was encrusted.

Further cleaning revealed carved designs on the bits that stood proud. They looked as if they had been overlaid with silver so that they would stand out against the dark ironwork a fraction of an inch beneath. The knuckle guard itself was fashioned into entwined leaves and deformed in the middle, pushed in towards the grip as if by a sharp blow. The ovoid pommel was fluted, solid and unadorned but the grip was the most difficult to clean because of the silvered twist-wire I could feel beneath the dirt. Eventually it all came up nicely enough, without appearing overdone, but there was still nothing to indicate ownership.

I was not disappointed; most swords had no such indication. What Shakespeare would most likely have wanted, and been prepared to pay for, was the best sword he could buy that was appropriate to his status. What we know of him – and we know quite a bit compared with what we know of most of his contemporaries – suggests that although status mattered significantly, he did not seek undue attention for himself. Doing what he did, he cannot have been a shrinking violet, of course; accounts indicate that he was sociable and agreeable but never one of the roistering boys. Money and security obviously mattered but the upstart crow seems never to have donned the plumes of the strutting cockerel. I would have liked the man, I told myself as I posed late that night before my bedroom mirror, sword in hand. A little unconvincing in striped pyjamas, perhaps, but the weapon handled nicely despite its length and weight. I kept it with me overnight rather than risk leaving it in the shop, laying it within reach on the carpet by my bed as if ready for action.

In the morning I posed with it again, slashing this way and that, pointing and stabbing. It was hard to imagine Shakespeare fighting, sword in one hand, dagger in the other, but I fancied that in the right clothes I might cut a threatening enough image. Less than dashing, admittedly, but purposeful, as if I meant it. After only a minute or two the weight of the sword made itself felt but the thought that my hand clasped what his had clasped – almost certainly, I was convinced – gave me strength. There is life in things we touch and use, something of ourselves clings to them.

I waited until after eleven to ring Charlotte, not wanting to appear too keen. 'Bring it this evening,' she said, 'at about eight. Don't eat. I'm cooking supper.'

Male vanity is impossible to underestimate but it is surely not unreasonable to speculate that a married woman who invites you to dinner when her husband is away may have something in mind. Nothing blatant, perhaps, but possibly the creation of circumstances in which I could be induced to feel that I was the seducer. If so, would I oblige? I found her attractive and had no moral qualms about deceiving Gerald. My reservations were the selfishly practical ones I had mulled over already: would an affair make it more or less difficult to secure the sword? How would it affect my business in our small community if it came to light? What if she, seeking a closer and more permanent relationship and suspecting I wanted the sword more than I wanted her, became embittered, went public, caused scenes? There is nothing I hate more than scenes.

Desire is of course a complicating factor. Mine was what might be expected of a middle-aged man in reasonable health who had grown accustomed to celibacy in recent years; hardly torrential, therefore, and with little danger of it breaching the dam of self-interest. But it was there; she was an attractive middle-aged woman with striking eyes and a figure that was lasting well. It helped significantly that she appeared to find me attractive, and it was pleasing to anticipate a modest revival of those carnal pleasures that had once been a principal preoccupation.

Of course, I should have asked myself why such a presentable woman would find an overweight, ageing shopkeeper with thinning hair and well-ploughed features an exciting proposition. But few of my gender are prone to such critical self-examination. Even if I had been, I should probably have concluded there was no accounting for taste, and felt grateful for it.

'Where?' Stephanie asked when I said I was dining out that night. When I told her she added, 'I like her.'

'She's very nice.'

'Can I come?'

'Not this time. Another time.'

She laughed. 'I would like that.'

For the first time for years that night I dithered about what to wear. I no longer had any idea about what might be appropriate to seduction. Perhaps it should be something neutral and relaxed that suggested nothing, made no statement, in case her intentions were not what I thought. Predictably, I settled for the sort of thing I always wear – corduroys and tweed jacket, checked shirt, no tie. *Better not to appear presumptive*, I thought. Anyway, unless I wore a city suit or dinner jacket, there was nothing else. It's years since I stopped wearing jeans, having concluded they make older men look as if they're trying too hard to look like younger men.

She received me wearing a blue silk dress, tight-waisted, flared from the hips and high-shouldered with a suggestive but not too revealing neckline. The blue enhanced her eyes, like the necklace she had worn before, only this time her necklace was a thin gold chain matched by another on her wrist. Her wedding ring was a thick gold band and her engagement ring a triple sapphire set in gold. Gerald had not stinted. I took the dress to be a positive indicator, implying accessibility.

Unwrapping the sword from its blanket, I handed it

to her, hilt first, with a mock bow. She took it with her right hand, balancing the blade on her left. 'It's beautiful. I had no idea it would clean up so well. Gerald will be impressed.'

'He might ask how you did it.'

'That's all right, I decided to tell him I had taken it to you for cleaning. Best to keep things as close to the truth as possible, don't you think?' She raised her eyebrows. 'He rang this afternoon. When I told him he just said he couldn't see the point in cleaning a dirty old poker. I said that was precisely why, because it was dirty. I didn't mention that you were coming to dinner. Would you like to see the cellar?'

Drinks in hand, we descended a steep flight of narrow brick steps behind the door under the stairs I had taken to be a cupboard. There, beneath a single dim bulb, were stacked Windsor chairs, armchairs, dismantled beds, chests of drawers, tables and smaller items, enough to fill a small barn of the sort commonly rented by my trade. It was mostly nineteenth- or turn-of-the-century stuff interspersed with a little Georgian, the lumber room of a family that had downsized in successive generations but couldn't bring itself to throw anything away. There were also stacks of old books.

'How did you get it down here?' The door and the stairs were narrow.

'There.' She pointed to the back of the cellar where,

in the gloom, I made out wider brick steps leading up to a double trapdoor at the front of the house, like many in Winchelsea. Beside the steps, against the wall, were three large wooden chests.

'What's in those?'

'Goodness knows, just old papers and things.'

'Family papers?'

'Letters from the outposts of empire. Such great letter-writers, the Victorians.'

'Older papers too?'

'Probably, I've never been through them.'

I stared at the chests as though staring might make their contents visible. There could be seventeenth-century papers pertaining to the sword and the Combes. I would have to get at them.

'This is what I was telling you about,' she said. She opened a violin case on a nearby table. The instrument was resonant with the patina of age. 'Beautiful, isn't it? It had all the Coombses fooled for centuries apparently until one of them – Gerald's uncle, I think it was – took it to an expert. Although it's only a copy of a Stradivari it's apparently a very good violin. No idea who played it. They're not at all a musical family.' She brushed the strings with her forefinger. 'But it's that sword that interests you, isn't it?'

'As you know. Not for its value or beauty or age or because I'm an obsessive' – I paused for her to reflect my smile – 'but because of its provenance. Possible provenance.' There was no point in holding back now, as we were already conspiring together, but I didn't want to overdo it.

'You really think it could have been Shakespeare's?'

'Could have, might have, possibly, just.'

'I love Shakespeare, I'm passionate about him.'

She had never shown any other sign of her passion but I wasn't going to argue. As I followed her back up the steps – did she exaggerate the swaying of her hips and the swing of her dress, or was it the stirring of lustful imagination? – I began telling her all I knew of the Combe family and of swords in Shakespeare's day. This continued over the mushroom omelette – she had warned me it would be a light supper – at the kitchen table with a bottle of white wine. The sword, meanwhile, she had laid not in the hearth but on the sofa.

'It's too good to be a poker again,' she said. 'It should be on the wall with the others.'

'Would Gerald permit that?'

'Of course not. Everything must always remain exactly as it was. Change frightens him, represents loss of control. I used to think this was just a male thing, made worse by the impotence of age, but now I think it goes deeper than that. With him, anyway. I suspect he was like it as a child. He certainly was in his working life. He usually left his job when he was asked to make changes or when change happened around him.

Odd thing is, he was sometimes appointed in order to bring about change.'

She spoke confidently and fluently now without the concluding giggle that always made her sound as if she was withdrawing what she'd just asserted. She sounded familiar with her thoughts, not needing to feel her way. I asked how they met.

'At a wedding. Dangerous things, weddings. Too many unforeseeable consequences.' She smiled. 'And you? How did you meet your former wife?'

I trotted her along the well-trodden path of my marriage and divorce, making light of the whole thing. I didn't want to waste time on myself. Apart from distracting from my purpose, it would have led to the charade of self-analysis, invariably the more self-serving and futile the more protracted it is. One is what one does and the rest is talk, which means excuse or concealment. 'I saw a rocking horse in the cellar,' I said, turning the subject back to them. 'But you've no children?'

'His grandfather's rocking horse. No, no children.' She shrugged. 'Perhaps just as well. We tried, or I did. Awful phrase. There was a time when I couldn't walk past a shop selling baby things without crossing the road, it so upset me. But it passed. It never bothered you, not having children?'

'No.'

'I didn't think it would have.'

Had I been more interested in myself, or in what others thought of me, I might have probed that. As it was, I was more struck by the different Charlotte that was showing through, the glint of sun on steel through the sea-mist indicating cannon on a man-o'-war rather than the unarmed merchantman I had supposed. But I was not then concerned to explore, being too concerned with whether or not we were supposed to be seducing each other as a preliminary to my acquiring the sword.

'Tell me about Stephanie,' she said. 'What exactly is wrong with her, if that's the right way to put it? What is her condition?'

I had discovered that talking about Stephanie was a good way of making myself appear agreeable and caring. Perhaps I am caring, up to a point, at least where Stephanie is concerned; but not in general.

'So she's perfectly happy doing cleaning and that sort of thing?'

'She loves cleaning.'

'She'd be welcome here with her duster. We have a daily – well, a weekly, really – but there's always more than she can get round to, with all our clutter. And I hate housework. I'd happily pay her, if you think she'd like to come over.'

'She'd love it.' It could be very helpful, not only for Stephanie, who really would enjoy it once she was used to being in a new place, but for me because I'd have to drop her off and pick her up and maybe hang around a bit. This prompted a new idea about the sword.

'We have an annex, a sort of granny flat built onto the side of the house,' Charlotte continued. 'You probably haven't noticed because you have to go past the front door and through a gap in the hedge. It's never used but it's very nice. She could stay in it if you or she wanted.'

'That might be very convenient, once she was used to being here.'

'That's what I was thinking.' There was an amused light in her eyes as they rested on mine.

We finished the wine between us, though I drank most of it. Afterwards we took our coffees into the drawing room where she sat at one end of the sofa, leaving the rest to the sword and an armchair to me. The message was clear, which was fair enough because my new plan for acquiring the sword did not depend upon intimacy with Charlotte. I had decided to substitute it. I would find another of the same period and similar style, work on it to make it look like the original, then discreetly substitute it. I wished I'd thought of this before cleaning it since I'd exposed a lot of detailing which would make it more difficult to find one with similar patterning of the hilt. But it was unlikely that the Coombses would pay it much attention, especially if I encouraged them to continue using it as a poker so that it became blackened and dirty again. If I'd thought of it when I had the sword in the shop I could have quickly bought the first rapier I came across and returned it as the cleaned-up version and they'd never have been any the wiser.

While I was thinking this she moved on to the pros and cons of living in Winchelsea, the factions and jealousies to be found in all allegedly close-knit communities, the difficulty of keeping anything private. I was half-listening but was recalled from my musings when she placed her cup onto the saucer with a decisive clink and then stood. 'What do you want?' she asked.

I stood, taking my time over it as I struggled for an answer. Were we reverting to seduction after all? How was I supposed to respond? I tried a smile. 'In general or—?'

'Not generally, or not entirely.' She nodded at the sword on the sofa. 'It's plain that you want that, your eyes have hardly left it since we came in here. What I meant was, what else do you want?'

'In life or just—?'

'I mean, is it just the sword? In which case, you can't have it. But if you want it badly enough to want everything that comes with it, we might find a way.'

I apprehended her meaning without quite believing it. We stood within touching distance, eyes fixed on each other's. Hers again had that strange light which might have been playful, or might not. 'What I mean,'

she continued slowly, 'is that you can have everything.'
She paused. 'But only everything.'

She was the Snow Queen, beguiling, untouchable.
'I'm not sure how we could arrange that.' We were
already speaking of it as a transaction.

With a shrug and another glance at the sword, she
turned and led the way back into the hall. 'That's what
you have to decide.' She opened the front door for me.

'Thank you for dinner,' I said. 'And for food for
thought.'

She leaned forward, brushed my lips with hers and
then firmly closed the door on me.

Chapter Five

I once read an account by an MI6 man called George Hill who had spied in Russia during the 1917 revolution and who, chased through the streets, ran one of his pursuers through with his swordstick. He made good his escape but paused a few streets away to examine his swordstick, noting 'only a slight film of blood halfway up the blade and a dark stain at the tip'.

That had the ring of truth for me. One would stop. It would be irresistible, just as a dog goes on sniffing at a rat it's killed but doesn't want to eat. This and related thoughts never left me during the next fortnight, prompted by the ever-present memory of the sword on the sofa, clean and deadly, ready for use. Presumably it was back in the hearth now. Normal life continued – I opened the shop, closed the shop, bought a little stock, sold less, lived with Stephanie. My obsession – as Charlotte would have it – with the sword did not eclipse consideration of her but it kept her somewhat to the rear of the stage, for some reason always slightly out of focus. I found it difficult to picture her precisely. If I had apprehended her meaning correctly – it was hard to put any other construction on it – she was offering me the sword on condition that I also took on her, the house and everything else. Except, presumably, her husband. Such deals may be proposed more often than we think but they are rarely so explicit. Life, including personal relations, is a series of transactions, but we don't like to admit it. Shopkeeping is more honest.

In the darker reaches of my apprehension I was aware of the implication that Gerald would somehow have to be removed from the scene, but I did not admit it fully to consciousness. Nor did I know how far she shared my apprehension. Did she have a plan or was she just vaguely aware that something would have to be done but preferred to leave it to me? That was perhaps part of the reason for the lack of focus when I tried to picture her, a symptom of my inability to fathom her. Except that I could always picture the playful, equivocating light in her eyes. But what was she playing with – her proposition, me, herself? Did she actually want the physical relationship with me she appeared to offer or was it merely a bargaining chip to be dangled as a prospect before me? In which case, how could she be so confident that I would want such a relationship that she was prepared to reveal herself so completely? Whatever my desires, my reactions had been – I hoped – outwardly as cool as hers. Perhaps her belief in her powers of attraction was such that she simply assumed all men wanted her. Or was it a phenomenon I had occasionally observed in both sexes: the fire of her own desire burned so bright that it seemed to her to set any man aglow with the same flame?

Or was she, like me, at once attracted and undecided, while, unlike me, lacking any equivalent of the sword to bring her on? Yet the manner of her proposal hardly smacked of indecision. Maybe she did have an equivalent of the sword: her determination to rid herself of Gerald.

Then, on a Tuesday afternoon, they both came into the shop. I was engaged with a customer interested in my seventeenth-century lantern clock, the one that had remained unsold since the day I bought the shop. He was the only person to have shown any interest in it apart from the solitary collector, the obsessive who had lectured me on it. This man was no expert. I had told him it needed restoration, that it wasn't a Richard Savage but was probably of his school. He was mulling over whether to buy it and have me restore it at unknown cost or buy it as seen and get it done himself. I was reluctant to break off, so when the Coombses entered I acknowledged them with no more than a nod. Charlotte smiled and turned to my silverware cabinet. Gerald stood monumentally where she had left him, in the middle of the shop, staring at the long-case clock without a face, each seemingly as blank as the other.

'Where's the best place to take it if I have it done myself?' asked the customer.

'Bill Bruce in Lewes. One of the best in the country.'

'If you have it restored, where would you send it?'

'Bill Bruce.'

'You don't know anywhere else?'

'It's not worth a quick fix, by which I mean it's worth much more than a quick fix which would work out dearer in the end anyway. Either do it properly or not at all.'

He nodded and bent again to examine the workings, breathing loudly through his nose like the doctor I used to be sent to as a child. I could tell he didn't really know what he was looking at but wanted me to think he did. He probably sensed a bargain if he made a low offer for it as it was. Well, he would be wrong there. I excused myself for a moment and went over to Gerald.

Incongruously for the mild weather, he was wearing a tweed shooting jacket and deerstalker. I was about to attempt a feeble joke by offering to sell him gun and boots but decided against it on seeing his face. He stared at the empty clock, his red cheeks unmoving, his eyes fixed, his lips slightly parted. He reminded me of a stuffed bear – Byron's, I think it was – I had once seen in an exhibition at the V&A Museum many years ago. Except that Gerald was taller.

'The works have gone off for repair,' I told him. 'It's a fine clock, a reputable maker, but not as rare as your local piece, your Bourn clock. We must arrange a time for me to come over and fix that chime.'

There was no response. For a moment I wondered whether I had spoken or whether I had imagined I had, mistaking the intention for the act. Then, incrementally, like an old ship of the line slowly changing tack, signs of life and recognition flickered fitfully across his features and he turned towards me. He turned his whole body, not just his head. 'Father won't have it.'

'He wouldn't like it? Your father wouldn't like it if I stopped the chimes?'

'Father's dead.'

'Yes, I—'

'Chap coming over to do the chimes. Simon Gold. Knows all about chimes.'

Charlotte came between us, her hand on his arm. 'It's all right, darling, this is Simon. He knows about that. We will arrange for him to come over.' She turned to me, her eyes urgent with appeal. 'He's a little confused today, often happens when he's getting a cold. Could you come tomorrow, after you've closed? And bring Stephanie, if she likes the idea.'

The unlikely customer was holding the lantern clock

aloft now, peering up at it. I didn't trust him with it. I nodded to them both as I went back to him. 'I shall, yes. About six.'

The man left a while later, saying he would think about it and call back. He never did, of course.

Stephanie laughed when I told her what we were doing that evening. 'Will Millie be there?'

'Who is Millie?'

'Millie lives there.'

It turned out that Millie was Charlotte's cat and that Charlotte had promised to introduce Stephanie to her. I had not seen Millie but remembered warily noticing a water bowl on the kitchen floor – warily because I can't abide cats, whereas Stephanie loves them and longs to have one. I suffered occasional spasms of guilt for not permitting it – it would be a daily delight for Stephanie – but I really didn't want to share the flat with a feline. It's something to do with their furtive predatory presence and the way those pale merciless eyes follow you everywhere; you know very well that if you were smaller they would kill you and eat you. Besides, they make me sneeze.

'I expect Millie will be there,' I said. 'Also, Charlotte may have some work for you to do, some cleaning work.'

Stephanie stared, open-mouthed and dismayed. 'I want to work here.'

'You will, we won't leave here. But I could take you to Charlotte's house to do some cleaning once or twice a week. You'd like that, wouldn't you?'

'I want to work here.' She was on the verge of tears.

'You will, Steph, it's all right. We'll go there together and we'll see Millie. And Charlotte will pay you, too. She will give you money. But we don't have to do it at all, not if you don't want to.'

She stood still, watching me shut the shop. 'I do want to,' she said eventually. We both smiled.

When we arrived Stephanie was reluctant to get out of the car. I got her along the garden path to the front door only by walking alongside with my arm around her. 'Are you going to stay here?' she asked.

'Yes, I'll be here all the time. It's all right.' When Charlotte opened the door we saw a black cat curled up on the stairs behind her. 'Stephanie is very much looking forward to meeting Millie,' I said.

Charlotte caught on immediately, smiling and taking Stephanie's hand. 'Yes, of course, and here she is, waiting for you.' She led her to the stairs where Stephanie, encouraged by Charlotte, tentatively stroked the creature.

It was either asleep or indifferent, making no response at all. Stephanie turned to me with a beatific smile. 'She lets me stroke her.'

From then on all was well. Charlotte scooped up the

cat and put it in Stephanie's arms. We all went into the kitchen where Stephanie stood holding it and smiling, and smiling.

Charlotte turned to me. 'Drink first or clock first?'

'Clock.'

As we passed the drawing room she poked her head in. 'Asleep,' she whispered. 'Or reading the paper. Same thing. Seems to sleep more and more now.'

'Is he unwell?'

'No more than usual.'

It was the work of minutes to disconnect the chime but I cleaned and examined the rest of it while listening to Charlotte instructing Stephanie downstairs on minor cleaning tasks. Stephanie sounded happy with everything provided Millie was in the room. The clock, as I had suspected, was a pretty crude and simple mechanism, assembled from bought-in parts. But nearly two hundred years later it was still going. I wound it, set it and left it ticking evenly.

At the bottom of the stairs I crept into the drawing room. The sword was back in the hearth with the other implements. The fire was laid but the blade was as clean as when I returned it, so it had not yet resumed its poker services. Gerald was asleep in the far armchair, legs outstretched, one foot crossed over the other, head back, mouth open, a copy of the *Daily Telegraph* spread across his torso. He wore a checked shirt with a dark-red tie, matching slippers, calf-length black socks and no trousers. A white towel was draped across his knees and thighs.

I stepped back into the hall to find Charlotte observing me from the kitchen door. 'I'm sorry, I—'

'Don't worry, you won't have woken him. I gave him something before you came. He'll be out for half an hour or so and then he'll go to bed.'

'You slipped something in his tea?'

She nodded and smiled. 'Come outside and I'll explain.'

Stephanie was sitting at the kitchen table cleaning a pile of silver cutlery with Millie curled up on the chair next to her. She was working on a dessert spoon, slowly and laboriously as always when she polished. She was good with silver, taking an unconscionable time but eventually achieving a deep shine. She put down the spoon and solemnly put her finger to her lips when we entered. 'Millie's sleeping.'

'Just like Gerald,' said Charlotte. 'I'm just going to show Simon something in the garden. You'll be all right looking after Millie, will you? We won't be long.'

'You have a way with her,' I said when we were outside. 'She wouldn't normally accept being left in a strange house.'

'I've had to get used to people who need looking after.'

'I couldn't help noticing that when you were in the shop Gerald—'

'Yes, I want to talk to you about that.' She led the way through the gap in the hedge to the annex she had mentioned, a narrow, weatherboarded, one-up-one-down cottage attached to the house. 'Stephanie could stay here, it could be her quarters if she ever – if she feels happy about staying overnight sometimes.' Her nervous tinkling laugh had reappeared. 'But, yes, with Gerald it's – it's early onset, I suppose that's what you'd call it. It's what the doctor said, anyway. Dementia, I mean.' She looked down at the small patch of lawn fringed with flowerbeds in front of the annex. 'What a state. Our gardener hasn't been near this for weeks. He must have forgotten about it. As had I until now. He comes tomorrow. I'll tell him.'

I stared at the lawn, too, but without noticing anything about it. 'You mean, Gerald has dementia already, now?'

'Yes, I suppose that's what I do mean, yes.' She turned back to me and giggled again. 'It comes and goes. He seemed better in recent weeks, quite his old self. Not that he was ever very ... but now he's suddenly much worse. He got lost the other day. The police found him. He wandered off from here without me knowing and walked all the way down to Winchelsea beach and carried on walking into the sea, fully clothed. For a while I thought – I almost hoped – you know ...' She still smiled but no sound came.

'Why is he wearing no trousers now? Incontinence?'

'No, not that, not yet, thank goodness. He forgot, simply forgot to put them on. I didn't tell him because he gets so annoyed when I try to point things out that I feared there'd be a scene when you arrived and that it would scare Stephanie off. It wasn't long before you came. If he wakes up and notices he'll go and put them on and then he might be perfectly all right for the rest of the evening. Most of it, anyway.'

'How awful for you. For you both.' The latter was an afterthought.

'Yes, it is, rather.' Unsmiling now, she looked at me as if expecting something from me. I was about to ask whether she had any plans for if – when – Gerald became unmanageable, when she resumed with her earlier crisp decisiveness. 'I've been thinking of something which, if it appeals to you, would resolve the situation for me – and for him – and would get you what you want.'

'What is that?' I didn't really need to ask but didn't want to admit that to myself.

'Kill Gerald.'

I had learned – too late in life to take advantage of it – that if you don't press your desires upon a woman, and you give her time, she will make hers plain, and that that simplifies everything. You merely have to be receptive and attentive. Charlotte spoke those two short words as quietly and mildly as if correcting me over the name of a plant. Her face was framed by small pink roses growing against the white weatherboarding behind her and her words were accompanied by bird-song from somewhere.

I didn't pretend to be shocked because I wasn't. It seemed natural to take the lead from her in approaching it as a purely practical matter. 'Is that really necessary? After all, if his dementia—'

'It is if you want the sword.'

I nodded. Already I was deceiving her, thinking how much simpler and less risky was my substitution plan. For that I would need continuing access to the house, however, so it was necessary to pretend to go along with her.

'And what comes with it,' she continued. 'All this' – she indicated the house and garden – 'and me.' She spoke now with the faintest smile and a slight lift of her eyebrows.

I returned her smile, marvelling inwardly at how easily she moved from her giggling, gushing social persona to this cool and intimate clarity. 'The question is how,' I said. 'It would require careful planning.' Which would take time, I did not add, time in which Gerald might die anyway, or walk off a cliff next time he strayed. Time, too, for me to find a substitute sword.

'That's for you to work out.' She turned back through the gap in the hedge.

*

It took weeks to locate a rapier similar in period and style to Shakespeare's. Internet searches, phone calls, visits and viewings, ploughing through catalogues were all unavailing. There were later swords in abundance and even earlier medieval weapons – big two-handed pieces – were not in short supply. But swords designed to be worn in daily or official life came in only during the later sixteenth century and were falling out of regular use by the end of the next. There were plenty in museums but few for sale. Finally, I remembered Stuart Gillingham, whom I had met years before on a furniture restoration course at West Dean College. He wasn't on my course – he taught metalworking – but we got to know each other and kept in touch after he left to set up his own craft smithy near Chichester. We did occasional business together. He was a real master craftsman and as sharp as some of his products when it came to doing a deal. Because of that I didn't warn him of my interest but drove over one afternoon and dropped in.

He had aged since we last met – more stoop, less hair, his face more pinched. Presumably I had aged too but that was harder to believe. Things outlive men and his workshop was as I remembered, full of tools, jigs, lathes, anvils and works in progress. Stuart is one of those increasingly rare craftsmen who, if he doesn't have a part for something, be it a clock, an engine, a barometer or a pump, will set to and make one. Unlike our modern throwaway culture, this ethic of repair has for me an atavistic appeal, as a link with our ancestors.

'What do you want with one of them things?' he asked when I explained. 'Got a customer with more money than sense? S'pose they must have if they come to you.' He laughed. 'I don't keep that sort of stock any more. No point with all these modern imitations they turn out in China or India or wherever. No matter that it's rubbish steel if they're never put to use.' He shook his head, squinting. 'Could make one for you. Do you a nice one.'

It would be, I was sure, but I had more sense than money and anyway couldn't wait for the months he would probably spend on it. 'You haven't any old bits and pieces knocking around? Cobble something together?'

'Have a rummage if you like.' We went down into his cellar, a brick-lined cavern of metal and junk, larger than Gerald's. 'You stay where you are. Don't want anything moved. I know where everything is down here. Don't believe me, do you?'

I did. He was that kind of man, cantankerous or helpful according to the day, his mood, the cut of someone's jib. He would refuse to sell to anyone he took against, just as he had refused to speak to pupils he thought weren't serious.

Minutes later he emerged from behind a couple of grey government-issue security cabinets holding half a rapier, its blade snapped off a foot or so from the point. 'This do you?'

It was even more battered and discoloured than Shakespeare's – as I now invariably thought of it – and the decoration on the swept hilt was different. But it was a similar shape to his and had an unbroken cross-guard. The handle felt like coiled wire, as with Shakespeare's, but the pommel was squared off rather than ovoid. What was left of the blade showed a single fuller or groove running two-thirds of the length of it. With a new blade and with alterations, it might just pass. Gerald, uninterested, would almost certainly not notice. Getting it past Charlotte, now that she had seen it cleaned and knew of my interest, would be harder.

'Might do. Might.' I sounded as doubtful as I could, for the sake of my wallet. 'Just. If you could make up a new blade or fit another old one. Any old iron will do but without the fuller and with, if possible, a ridge. Also without the curved bottom end of the cross-guard. Break that off.'

He took it back from me, looking at it closely. 'Want a lookalike, do you? Someone's got a twin and wants to put it on his wall?'

'That sort of thing.'

'I could weld another bit of blade on but it would show if you look closely and the steel would be differ-ent. Also this has a fuller. Better dismantle it and make a complete new blade.'

'So long as you can distress it, make it look old. And clean up the handle and guard and round off or replace the pommel. He'd like an ovoid.'

Stuart's little eyes twinkled. 'Very particular, your customer, is he? Or won't he know it's been bodged?'

'He wants to hang it on his wall with another, as you surmised. He wants an identical pair.'

'Bring me the other one and I'll make them into a pair.'

'He's not that fussed about accuracy and he's in a hurry. Wants them for when he moves into his new house. How soon can you do it?'

'Instant ancestral mansion, eh? Anything's possible if he's prepared to pay for it.'

And, being Stuart, he made me pay through the nose. But he promised it in a week or two.

Coaxing Stephanie into cleaning for Charlotte a couple of times a week proved easier than I had thought. In fact, she needed no coaxing. Charlotte fussed over her and made her laugh and Millie became the passion of her life. She still is. During each of these visits Charlotte and I would contrive time alone together, not quite as lovers' trysts but they felt like it. It was almost as if, in assuming we would be lovers one day, we had got beyond that. In fact, we used those times for plotting. I was happy to prolong plotting for as long as possible, of course – at least until I had the replacement sword – and so eagerly discussed with her the various methods of disposal, as we called it.

I realise now that words are not merely labels for thoughts but that they embody the thought, they are the thought incarnate. If you don't have the word for it you can't think it and if you do have a word it is the word that determines how you think of it. Thus, when calmly discussing how best to dispose of Gerald – a living, breathing being, as warm with life as ourselves – we talked as if he were recyclable waste. And because we talked of him like that, we came to see him as that; which, of course – along with the rest of us – is what ultimately he was.

The other feature of those discussions was their erotic charge. Conspiracy, a secret shared, stimulates the erotic. When a man and a woman between whom there is already a half-acknowledged – or mutually feigned – attraction conspire together in a private place, it is hard to be indifferent to the possibilities. Most of our discussions were while she was supposedly showing me round the annex or cottage that Stephanie was to occupy, where it would have been easy to jump into bed together if we'd cared to chance it. But we did not. She indicated her awareness in small ways, a half-smile here, a lift of the eyebrows there, a shrug, an intonation, a playful glance. Being suggestive, these little signs were more erotic than any sudden clinching or groping for each other's genitalia.

But I could never quite make up my mind whether she was doing it to make me want her or because she thought it was what I expected, and she needed to keep me engaged. I did want her, up to a point, but held back because I was unsure of her. Was she really serious about killing Gerald? Was she mad? Was she playing a game I couldn't fathom? Did she really want me or not?

The result of this mutually teasing restraint was that the erotic energy generated was diverted into plotting. We discussed schemes and methods as eagerly as if we were planning a surprise party. It felt it had nothing to do with Gerald.

We considered bludgeoning, poisoning, shooting, stabbing, running over. My favourite was that she should take him for a walk on Fairlight Cliffs in the dusk and push him off, claiming he'd slipped and fell. So long as there were no witnesses, no one could prove otherwise. But she claimed he was too big and heavy for her to push and it might only half-work, leaving him alive to tell the tale. In fact, I suspect she didn't want to do it herself. The problem with virtually all other methods was disposal of the body, leaving us to conclude that either he had to disappear and never be found or his death had to look like an accident. Eventually, we settled on a combination of both: given that the police had already been involved in rescuing him from the sea, and so knew him to be liable to wander, we should try to arrange a repeat performance with, this time, no rescue.

Once, when we'd discussed for the third time how we might get him to the water's edge unseen, I asked her for how long she had been thinking of murdering her husband. I hadn't planned to but she seemed relaxed and I had often wondered about it. I didn't put it too bluntly, phrasing it something like, 'How long have you been thinking of resolving your marital problem in this way?'

'Years. Since very soon after our marriage when I realised how unbearable he was to live with.'

'Wouldn't it have been simpler to leave him?'

'He couldn't cope, he'd be helpless on his own. He needs someone to look after him. He lived with his parents until I married him. Besides, I'd have felt so guilty.'

'And you wouldn't feel guilty now if we ... when we ...?'

She shook her head. 'In losing his life now he wouldn't be losing anything he's conscious of having. Well, he is in fits and starts but decreasingly. Quite soon he won't be aware of anything. He'll either wander off into the sea again and not be found – without our help – or he'll walk under a bus or something and possibly cause other people to be injured. We can't afford to put him in a home. I'm not a gaoler, this house wasn't built as a prison, I can't keep him in all the time. Even with your capable hands to help me.' She finished with another half-smile.

The obvious rejoinder, of course, was that if Gerald's self-removal was inevitable and imminent there was no need for us to dispose of him. We had only to wait. But I didn't want to suggest that until I had exchanged the swords.

I had a few brief solo encounters with Gerald during the weeks running up to his removal, mostly inconsequential and meaningless. He might be standing in the hall or drawing room when I arrived with Steph. He would often stand, unmoving and expressionless, for twenty minutes at a time, gazing at nothing. Or perhaps his gaze was inward, focused on we know not what in the thickening fog of his brain. Sometimes he would respond almost normally to my greeting but at others I might as well have greeted the wall.

There were two or three occasions he appeared to have recovered his normal self, albeit that wasn't perhaps very normal by most people's standards. Once, when he greeted me by name, shook my hand and thanked me for dropping by, I made the mistake of asking after the clock.

'Clock?' Fear and panic grew in his eyes. 'Very well, thank you, very well. Much better.' He turned and went into the drawing room, shutting the door behind him.

Another time we almost had a conversation in which

he nearly said something vital to my interests. It was a weekend and I was picking up Stephanie, who was reluctant to leave because Millie had gone out and couldn't be found and Stephanie wanted to say good-bye. Charlotte was trying to reassure her that Millie would be back soon and that Stephanie could leave a little something for her in her bowl.

Gerald came downstairs while this was going on. 'Ah, Mr Gold – Simon – good of you to call. I don't think I ever thanked you properly for taking that desk back. Rest assured I shall come to you next time I want anything.'

I began the usual self-deprecatory remarks but he cut me short. 'Yes, and that sword, that sword we've got that you were asking about, the one we use as a poker. Don't think I ever told you, did I? Must've slipped my mind—'

There was a squeal of delight from the kitchen as Stephanie greeted the return of Millie through the cat-flap. Charlotte turned to us both, smiling triumph-antly. Gerald stopped, glanced at her, then back at me. He stared now as if he couldn't place me, then nodded, smiled, patted me on the shoulder and turned back upstairs. That was the last time the three of us were together before his removal.

Chapter Six

Stuart Gillingham had my sword ready more or less within the agreed period but not within the agreed budget, which he now called an estimate. 'Worth a few bob extra for a blade that does the job,' he said. 'As long as you don't make me an accessory after the fact. Who you going to use it on, anyway?'

We laughed at that as I paid up. He had done a proper job: neither the blade nor the ovoid pommel looked new and you had to look very closely indeed to see that it had been joined. That could have happened at any time, anyway, since swords were often re-bladed. The cross-guard looked fine, broken just where Shakespeare's had been and looking as if it had been done a long time ago. If you had the two swords to compare, side by side, you would easily spot differences, but, apart, only someone with a real interest would be likely to spot them. If all went according to my plan, no one would ever see them together, anyway.

When I got the sword home I dented the knuckle guard a little more, using the small hammer I normally kept for picture-hanging. My next task was to effect the substitution undetected. It would not be easy because Stephanie and I were never alone there without Charlotte, who would anyway be contriving opportunities for us to plot the removal of the obstacle, as she now referred to Gerald. At such moments I still wondered which of us was mad, or whether both, though I always absolved myself by reminding myself that I didn't intend to go through with it. But for her, I really couldn't say. She didn't seem mad, as that imprecise term is conventionally understood. Everything else about her suggested a mind firmly – perhaps too firmly – planted in everyday reality. It was only when it came to discussing the disposal of the obstacle that there seemed to be a disconnect from the normal. Maybe she was unusually honest, voicing what many half-think but never articulate, even to themselves. It was easy to see that years of living with Gerald might have made her desperate, but she always seemed especially calm and logical when discussing the subject. Perhaps that was it – perhaps she was only logical, and that was where real madness lay. Eileen, their GP friend whom I had made such an effort to get on with because I disliked her so much, might have an opinion. But I daren't confide.

An opportunity for action came the following week. Charlotte told me she had to take Gerald to the hospital for half a day of memory tests on a day that Stephanie was due to clean. She asked whether I would be able to close the shop to be with her or whether she would cope alone in the house. Postponing her, she realised, was likely to be very upsetting. I said I'd bring Stephanie over and see how she got on, closing the shop if necessary. Charlotte gave me a spare key, saying, with a smile, 'This feels pleasingly naughty, doesn't it?'

When the day came I didn't want to be seen walking out of the shop sword in hand, even if it was wrapped in a blanket; nothing goes unnoticed in our part of town. I had a bag of Edwardian golf clubs in the shop, more as a stage-prop than seriously for sale, and so slotted the sword among them with a waterproof draped over the top. Just as well, since a neighbour from over the road, a man about my own age who told everyone he was an artist but never produced any-thing, came out as we were getting into the car. 'Didn't know you were a golfer, Simon?' he called cheerily. 'Locally or elsewhere?'

'They're antiques. Showing them to a customer.'

He laughed. 'Good luck with that.'

Stephanie's mind was fixed upon cleaning and the prospect of seeing Millie again. She neither saw the sword nor asked why I was bringing the clubs into the house. Charlotte had left instructions on the kitchen table that Stephanie was to start by vacuuming the kitchen and utility room. I left her fussing over Millie.

Alone in the drawing room with my bag of clubs, I closed the door and lay the two swords side by side on the carpet. They looked near enough the same sort of thing but they clearly weren't twins. You could have got away with showing them as examples of typical late-sixteenth- or early-seventeenth-century English rapiers influenced by continental fashion, possibly by the same hand. I hadn't realised until that moment, however, that Stuart's was a good three inches shorter than Shakespeare's. I was pretty sure I had given Stuart the measurements; perhaps Gerald wasn't the only one whose mind was going. Too late now, it would have to do.

For some minutes I indulged myself again with Shakespeare's sword, alone in that room under the disapproving gaze of Gerald's ancestors. I lunged and parried, drew from an imaginary scabbard, cut and swished. For a while I simply walked around the room, holding the sword before me and once more wishing, willing, that by some strange alchemy something of William Shakespeare would transmit itself through that slim grip.

Perhaps it did. His plays are full of abrupt exits and surprise entrances. The door opened to reveal Gerald staring at me, open-mouthed, his fist clasping the door handle. He wore a green tweed suit with a matching tie and yet another checked shirt. His jacket was undone – it wouldn't have met across his belly anyway – and in his other hand he held a tweed cap. I saw him only when I turned so he must have witnessed my last pirouette. The golf clubs and Stuart's sword were on the rug in front of the fire and I had just jumped over them.

We all know how selective and erratic memory can be. If you had asked me a couple of years ago I should have said that I spoke first, that I said something inane like, 'Forgive me, I was just trying out your swords, making sure they work.' But now I'm not so sure. I may have been about to say something like that, almost certainly I had thought of it, when Gerald forestalled me. He let go of the door and advanced into the room with slow steps, his face reddening. His glance took in not only me but Stuart's sword on the floor. He stopped in front of me, much too close for comfort, then shouted, 'Thief! You thief! You're a thief, sir! Damn thief!'

How he knew, I can't say, but some defunct mental connection had sparked back into life and he had divined my intention. His shout brought Charlotte into the room. 'We're back early,' she said, 'the appointment was—'

She stopped when she saw me with sword in hand and the other on the floor. From the kitchen came the sound of vacuuming. Gerald's lips worked and twitched but no sounds came now. I could smell his breath, warm and rank.

I stepped back from Gerald. I think I said 'no' a couple of times, adding, 'It's not like that.' I'm not sure he heard me because he turned away, stepping across Stuart's sword and the golf clubs and reaching for one of the military swords on the wall above the fireplace.

In recollecting a number of actions it's almost impossible to be sure one has the sequencing right. Things often happen simultaneously or so closely together that it's difficult afterwards to distinguish accurately between one's perceptions, one's intentions and one's actions. I'm confident that Gerald reached for the middle sword and that his intention was to grab it and use it, but whether to threaten or fight, or whether with some notion of necessary self-defence – though I wasn't threatening him – I don't know. I believe I said or shouted 'No!' again and may have added, 'Don't!' I think Charlotte said something, too. She may have said, 'Gerald!'

I stuck out my arm to stop him grabbing the sword. I did not want a sword fight. I hadn't forgotten I was holding Shakespeare's sword and I think my split-second intention was to interpose the blade between Gerald and the sword he was reaching for, rather as one might threaten with a walking stick. But he must have moved faster and farther than I thought because my point pierced his cheek. Newly sharpened as it was, it slid in easily. I felt no resistance.

I think we were as shocked as each other. He staggered back, dropped his cap and put his hand to his cheek, blood streaming between his fingers and over the back of his hand. But with his other hand he had grabbed the mortuary sword. I pulled my arm back and for a long moment we stared at each other. Then, like the MI6 man in the book, I looked at the tip of my blade. There was a small smear of red, not much, less than half an inch. I remember thinking, inconsequentially, 'I wonder if it's ever done that before.'

Gerald continued to stare as if I were doing or saying something of consuming interest. He no longer clutched his cheek, having lowered his hand, apparently oblivious of his bleeding. Then he raised his sword above his head, cutting edge towards me. I shouted – this I am certain of – 'No!' again, raising my left arm to protect myself and stepping back. At the same time I jabbed at him with my right arm, my sword arm, as if to deter or push him away. But of course the sword was still at the end of that arm. This time the long blade was lower and it entered his left shoulder about level with the top of his tweed lapel. There was a little more resistance than with his cheek but the point still slid in with disconcerting ease. It was not like a knife through butter, as the saying goes, more like pushing a sharp kitchen knife into a potato.

The effect was dramatic. He dropped the mortuary sword and staggered back a couple more paces, still open-mouthed, still staring. He said something – I think it was 'You' – and may have repeated it. Then his lips went bluish and his eyes widened as in surprise or outrage. His knees buckled and he fell heavily, knocking over a sidetable by one of the armchairs. The back of his head thumped on the floor. For a long moment Charlotte and I stood looking at him, then at each other. Stephanie's vacuum cleaning continued. I don't think it occurred to either of us to attempt to revive him, even had we known what to do. Then Charlotte smiled. 'Simon, darling, well done. That was brilliant.'

Chapter Seven

'I never thought you'd do it,' she said over a whisky the following evening. 'I really didn't.'

So far as I was concerned, I hadn't. She was crediting me with an intention I never had, though I could hardly deny the act. But I didn't tell her that because by then, as my sword's original owner wrote, I was 'in blood stepped in so far that, should I wade no more, Returning were as tedious as go o'er'. I find I read him more now than I did.

The evening of Gerald's – what? His accidental death? His disposal? His removal? His murder? – was busy, as you might imagine. Charlotte was the first to recover. While I was still holding the sword and wondering whether the charge would be murder or attempted murder or manslaughter and whether I could convince the police that the action which caused his heart attack was genuinely unintended, Charlotte was four or five steps ahead. She came up with a plan as if she had taken it fully formed from the shelf, laying down a path I have followed obediently ever since.

She held out her hand to me. 'Give me your sword. Don't touch him or his sword. I'll put it back on the wall. Take your golf clubs but leave the other sword, the new one, where it is. Go and take Stephanie home now. Don't let her in here, she mustn't see this. I'll tidy up while you're gone but when you've settled her come back and help me dispose of the body. Don't park outside the house and try not to let anyone see you return.'

I still wasn't with her, still thinking conventionally. 'But the police ...'

She smiled. 'Don't be silly, darling, we don't want the police to know about this, do we? Not until we're ready, and in our own way.'

It proved easier than I thought to get Stephanie out of the house. She had just turned off the vacuum cleaner as we entered the kitchen. Charlotte gushed over her, telling her what a wonderful job she'd done and suggesting tasks for her next visit while fetching her coat from the hall. She also asked – a brilliant touch, this – if Stephanie would cook a couple of rashers of bacon at home and bring them next time for Millie who loved bacon and hardly ever had it because Gerald couldn't bear the smell in the house. Stephanie was pleased but still a little nonplussed, since she normally stayed longer and did more, but she could see I had the car keys in hand and she was always easily swayed by Charlotte's extravagant attentiveness. She still is.

At home we had scrambled eggs for supper with salmon and mushroom, one of her favourites. I had to force myself to eat. Afterwards we cooked two rashers of bacon for her to take next time. When I suggested we both had an early night she said she wanted to look at cats on her iPad. I said she could take it to bed with her, something I don't often allow because she has been known to stay awake most of the night with it and is then crabby and uncooperative the next day. But I wanted no trouble that night and she went to her room meekly enough.

Luckily, her bedroom light went out after half an hour or so and I crept out of the flat. I don't worry about leaving her alone at night though normally I tell her and assure her that everything will be locked and safe. During the drive to Winchelsea I was tempted not to turn off into the town but to keep going and going, to Truro, Kendal, Halifax, anywhere. The images of my sword entering Gerald, the surprise in his eyes as his lips turned blue, the inertness of his body and then the emptiness of his eyes as they stared at the ceiling were permanently present. Nor did I even attempt to think about what we might do next. It was not mental paralysis, exactly, so much as a heightened dreamlike irresponsibility, as if I were on some drug. Already I was leaving everything to Charlotte.

I parked as she had suggested in a quiet adjacent street, though I might just as well have parked outside the house since the only sign of life apart from traffic on the main road below was my own footsteps. By now I felt as carefree as if I were just popping round for a drink. Perhaps it helps you do something serious if you're not thinking about it.

She met me at the door with her finger to her lips. The hall light behind her was turned off and she closed the door quietly. 'No need to advertise comings and goings,' she whispered. 'Is Stephanie all right?'

'Tucked up in bed.'

'So sweet.' She took my hand. 'Everything's ready. I just need your help with the rug. He's such a heavy old lump.'

The room was restored to order, sidetable and lamp righted, the mortuary sword back on the wall, Stuart's sword in the hearth with the other fire irons and a copy of *Country Life* open on the sofa. Even Gerald's body was neater, his feet parked together and his hands by his side as if lying at attention. The previous day's *Daily Telegraph* was spread beneath his shoulders and head. It had absorbed some blood but not much had flowed.

'Where's—'

'The other sword? Your sword. I've hidden it. That was the only one used, wasn't it? The only one likely to have traces of his blood and your DNA on it. It's quite safe, don't worry. And no one will notice the new one in its place. So clever of you to think of that.' She squeezed my hand. 'But try as I might I couldn't get him fully onto the rug by myself. I was always telling him not to eat so much.'

Gerald was lying partially on, partially off the hearth rug. 'Why do you want him on it?'

'So we can roll him up in it and carry him out to the car. Then we can get rid of him and it at the same time. It's got blood on it so we'd have had to get rid of it anyway. And I've never much liked it. Time we had a new one.'

My expression must have been eloquent of something because she smiled again and tugged at my hand, as she did with Stephanie. 'Don't you see, silly? We can't have him found here with sword holes in him, even though he died of a heart attack. You'd be in the most frightful trouble, wouldn't you, darling?'

I noted the move from plural to singular.

'Much better that he's found elsewhere,' she continued, 'in a state in which your swordplay would not be revealed. The sea is the answer, don't you think? So helpful that he wandered off the other week and was rescued by the police. They'll know he has a history of that sort of thing. What if he wanders off tonight, letting himself out without my knowledge, and simply doesn't come back? And when he is eventually found – if he is – there's only what the fishes and gulls haven't eaten. And the rug goes with him. Don't you think that would be best, darling?'

Her tone was light and cajoling as if she were trying to persuade me of the need for new curtains or the colour of the new rug. I don't recall agreeing but I certainly didn't disagree. Anything to get rid of the problem.

He was indeed a heavy old lump. I'm used to shifting furniture but furniture is usually tidy, it doesn't flop or roll. We edged him inch by inch onto the rug, with me at one point hoisting him by the feet, hooking them through my arms in order to lift his pelvis. The edges of the rug, which was long enough but not wide enough, only just met when we folded it over him. We had to get string from the kitchen to tie it round him, which meant lifting him and it. By the time we finished I was panting and sweating. 'I'll have to bring the car round. We'll never carry him to it.'

'We couldn't fold him into our Golf, crumple him up a bit?'

'It would be much more difficult.'

Despite panting as much as me, she managed a laugh. 'I always used to tell him he was unbending.'

'Yet who would have thought the old man to have had so much blood in him?'

'What?'

'Nothing. A quote from Shakespeare. I'll get my car.'

'I love Shakespeare, I adore him.' She still says that. I reversed my estate car into their drive. It was a

Volvo so I couldn't extinguish the driving lights but I did switch off the interior lights so that they wouldn't display to the world what we were doing when we had the tailgate open.

Getting him out of the house was worse than trussing him up. We started with each of us holding one end of the rug, she at the head and me at the feet. But she couldn't hold it, even on the straight bits. We swapped ends and, a foot or two at a time with frequent gasping rests, we got him out of the drawing room and along the hall to the front door. After a longer rest she opened the door and we began the ten-yard journey to the back of the car. It was tempting to drag him on the pebbles but that might have made too much noise, so we sweated, panted, strained and heaved. Once we dropped him, the thick carpet slipping through our weakened fingers.

'God, he's so awkward. I never did like him,' she whispered.

'Why did you marry him?'

'Another time.'

There was an anxious moment when a car drove slowly down the road, its headlights sweeping across the front of the garden and the Volvo. We lowered Gerald to the floor and crouched. I imagined the police cruising around looking for anything suspicious. But the car turned the corner away from us and stopped outside a house at the far end of the lane.

'The Witneys,' she whispered. 'The judge and his wife. You met them here, remember?'

The hardest part was to come, lifting his whole upper body high enough to get him onto the floor of the car. It took four or five goes and we finally managed it only with each of us either side of his head and shoulders and linking hands beneath. I'd let the back seat down but it was still hard work to slide him in. We had to bend the rug and his legs to close the tailgate.

'How long before rigor mortis sets in?' I asked.

'Don't know. All the more reason to hurry. I'll just lock the house and we'll go up to Fairlight Cliffs. That would be the best place, don't you think?'

'What if the police stop us for some reason? What would we say?'

'There's no reason they should, is there? Anyway, you hardly see them these days and if they ask what we're doing up there we can just say ... well, we're off to do what couples normally do on the cliffs at night.'

We were standing together behind the car and I could make out her smile in the dark. As she finished speaking she felt exploratively for my groin. It was so unexpected that at first I did nothing. Then I rested my palm on her bum and stroked her through her skirt. Whether it was a primitive urge to assert life in the presence of death that was arousing, or whether it was the thrill of the clandestine, I don't know. What I do know is that sex was a million miles from my own thoughts until she did that, but then awareness of her arousal aroused me and for the rest of that evening provided a parallel fantasy to the seeming unreality of what we were doing.

It wasn't far to the cliffs, a chalk outcrop east of Hastings that relieves an otherwise featureless coast. The wind was getting up and there were gusts of rain, which made it somewhat unlikely that an adulterous couple would go sporting in the gorse. All the way through the winding lanes to the cliffs she kept her hand on my thigh. On the tighter corners Gerald's body shifted slightly in the back.

Nor was it a good choice for anyone with a car and a heavy load. The coast road is some hundreds of yards from the cliff edge, to reach which you have to turn into the visitor centre, park and walk. Not surprisingly, we were the only car there at that time of night apart from a clutch of vehicles parked outside the former coastguard cottages, beyond which you couldn't drive. There was no question of parking and carrying Gerald, quite apart from the now-steady rain which would have made the rug – and presumably his tweed – even heavier. Even had we got there, I now remembered, the cliff edge was rarely sheer and we would have had to throw him impossibly far out to ensure he didn't roll onto a ledge or rock below. I had thought vaguely of this on the way up but had assumed Charlotte knew some accessible place.

'Can't say I do,' she said, sounding as if it was nothing to do with her. 'It's years since I've been up here. Can't remember much about it, to be honest. We'll have to go down to Pett Level where it's open beach and do it there. Pity because I thought if we could get him onto the rocks the waves would bash him about a bit.' She gave my thigh a squeeze. 'Come on, let's get down there.'

Rain and wind worsened as we followed the road inland, then looped back to the coast, this time at sea-level. There were a few houses, then a pub and a lifeboat station with access to the sea, but there was little chance of doing anything unseen there. After that came a high sea wall intersected every hundred yards or so by steps. We were no more likely to be able to lug Gerald up those steps and across the shingle to the sea than to drive the Volvo up and over the wall. Fortunately, there was little traffic to note us as we crawled along the sea road, stopping at the occasional concrete ramps allowing official vehicle access to the wall, each with a locked barrier at the bottom.

'Stop, go back, that one moved,' said Charlotte.

I got out to have a look. Sure enough, the plastic barrier hadn't been padlocked to its metal strut and was swinging to and fro with the wind. I walked up the ramp onto the wall, buffeted by wind, spray and rain as I crested it. The tide was up and, better still, the ramp led to a short stone breakwater or groyne just wide enough to take a vehicle. Waves were breaking over it at the far end and the water either side looked reasonably deep. An outgoing tide would be helpful.

'We must get him out of the rug,' said Charlotte when I reported back, dripping wet. 'We must dump that somewhere else. Don't want him found anywhere near it.'

I waited until an oncoming car had passed and then reversed through the swinging barrier and up the ramp. We would leave tyre tracks, perhaps, but they wouldn't last long. Once we were on the wall Charlotte opened the door to get out and watch me back, then promptly closed it.

'I can't go out in these clothes, they'll be ruined. It's awful out there. Have you anything I can put over it?'

I hadn't but reckoned I would manage. The reversing lights weren't strong enough for me to rely on wing mirrors so I had to open the window and stick my head out, squinting against the spray and rain blowing straight off the sea behind us. Slowly, keeping the car parallel to the edge of the groyne, I edged along it, leaving myself just enough room to get out.

'You stay here and I'll see if I can drag him out myself.'

'I don't think I could get out anyway, we're right on the edge this side, I'd go straight into the sea. Have you got something to cut the string with?'

'Yes.' I am the kind of person most people consider boring because I always go prepared, as Boy Scouts were supposed to. I don't mind that, I like boring things. If they still made them and I didn't need more room in a car I'd drive a Morris Minor. A penknife, tape measure, notepad and pen or pencil are necessities of my trade, even with the advent of smartphones. As I squeezed through the door the wind seemed to increase, buffeting and bullying with an almost personal spite. I clung to the door handles to steady myself. Volleys of spray showered me from the far end of the groyne, only a few yards beyond the car. When I opened the tailgate it jerked violently out of my hand as the wind got beneath it. I cut the string round the rug and began dragging Gerald out. It was nothing like as hard as getting him in but he remained to the end a solid, resistant lump.

'Are you sure you can manage?' Charlotte called when I had his feet on the ground and his head and shoulders still in the car. 'It's blowing wet in here with the back open.'

After more heaving his head thumped onto the wet stone. I remember thinking that that would have done for him if nothing else had. I pulled the rest of the rug out and closed the tailgate. Next thing was to drag him as near as I could get to the far end. That was hard, too. Everything was hard now. I could feel my corduroys wet against the backs of my legs and the flap of my jacket slapping against my back. Twice I nearly lost my footing before concluding I couldn't get to the end without serious danger of going in with him. He would have to go over the nearer edge, but even dragging him there was risky. It was too dark to see much of him apart from his bulky shape and large pale face. I knelt beside him and began trying to roll him. That too was hard work. I got his head and shoulders near the edge, then went to the other end and grabbed a foot to lever one leg over the other. His leg was heavy and while I was pulling it over his shoe came off in my hands and went into the sea. I rested for half a minute, still kneeling, my elbows on his hip. Then I pushed again, and again. Slowly at first, then with unstoppable momentum, the sodden bulk slid off the edge into the surly water below, leaving me kneeling as in prayer. The wind and waves were such that I heard only a muted splash.

I suppose we should really have taken the rug and string a mile or so along the coast to dump them but I was wet and exhausted and my hands weak with cold. I threw them both in on the other side of the groyne.

When I was back in the car she said, 'Well done, darling. I wish I could hold you on the way home but you're soaking. Where's the rug?'

I told her.

'It would have been better to separate them. We don't want it associated with the body.'

'They'll drift apart, surely. And the sea should take care of any blood or DNA. And there was nothing on it to say where it came from.'

'It was his father's, of course. Probably Persian but very worn and not a very nice one. I've been longing to replace it, as I said. Nice to think I can now.' As we neared Winchelsea the rain lessened and she said, 'Better not drop me near the house. Fewer sounds of movement the better. I'll just have to chance getting wet.'

'What will you … we …?'

She smiled. 'Don't worry, darling, everything's under control. You drive straight home and go to bed. Make sure you get the car valeted tomorrow and I'll make sure everything's tidied up in the house. First thing in the morning I'll call the police. I'll say I got up to go to the loo and saw his bed was empty and found the front door unlocked. Then I'll go and ask friends and neighbours, then later in the day I'll ring you as a friend and ask you to come over and help with the search. What we'll do next depends on when the body is found. If it's found.'

'But what about the—?'

'About the sword? Oh, that's already safe enough, don't worry. No one will find it and your replacement is in its place. No one will know the difference. So clever of you to think of that.'

I had stopped the car by then. She leaned across and again brushed my lips with hers. 'Be patient, darling, we'll soon be together properly.'

Chapter Eight

It all worked as she intended. The police search the next day, including dozens of volunteers, featured on local radio and television. There was an interview with a restrained and dignified Charlotte, who managed to convey deep emotional currents while staying calm on the surface and thanking all involved for their help. It was a finely wrought performance; I was proud of her.

The Military Canal, a defence structure dating from the Napoleonic Wars, runs along the foot of Winchelsea and is an obvious hazard for anyone out of his mind enough to wander into it. Police divers came and dragged it while volunteers walked the beach between Rye and Pett Level. A dead dog was found. A helicopter buzzed around and a lifeboat cruised up and down offshore until the wind got up again and the seething grey sea became querulous, at which point everyone gave up and went home. It was an impressive effort, all told.

I tried to imagine Gerald's body, a soggy mass tossed about in those waves, sinking a bit here, rising there. It would not incarnadine those multitudinous seas, as Shakespeare had it, but would be consumed utterly unless washed up somewhere. Presumably it would cease floating once all the air was out of it, the head and limbs would come apart and sea creatures would lunch on it. I tried too to feel something for the man the flesh had embodied. Not a bad man, surely. Never happy in himself, perhaps, not only unfulfilled but lacking any potential for fulfilment, with no gift for making others happy and little awareness of or sympathy for those around him. But not actively bad and his asking me to take Charlotte to concerts and talks suggested he must have sensed her longing for something other than the joy of living with him in his father's house. Unless she had put him up to it. But certainly not a bad man as men go, not cruel or brutal or dishonest, just not noticeably good, either. Something of a lost soul, as lost in life as his disintegrating remains were now in death.

I couldn't feel much for him because the decomposing mess wasn't him and whatever had been him was no more. He had been losing it, anyway, whatever was him. *Being dead would be all right*, I thought, *just like before you were born.*

Yet a better man than me, I now think.

Charlotte rang me late that afternoon, pretending to tell me for the first time what had happened. I acted my part, shocked and concerned, again admiring her act. 'It would be so nice if you could come over and help. Most of the searchers have gone now but I'd like to walk the ditches down by the station. We rarely went that way but Gerald and I had walked down there once or twice and it's possible he might have remembered.' I presumed she thought that phone calls might somehow be recoverable but she was also, I now realise, setting the tone for our subsequent life together.

Winchelsea Halt is on the single-track railway line traversing the valley between Hastings and Rye, near Dumb Woman's Lane. The River Tillingham runs through fields intersected by dykes and ditches which flood in winter and in which the frail or suicidal might plausibly drown. When I picked her up at the house she was already in Wellington boots, Barbour jacket and matching hat, with two of Gerald's walking sticks. 'I thought it would be sensible to involve you early on, in my hour of need,' she whispered. 'Makes it more natural that we get together later. I've told people you're coming to help and that we'll concentrate on the inland bits since everyone else has been searching coastwards. I've got a stick for you, look.'

We parked near the halt and enjoyed a wet ramble, probing ditches and pools with our sticks. We talked again about the long-threatened, ever-delayed bypass, agreeing that it would be criminal to ruin that valley, and about the disfiguring new windmills cluttered over towards Dungeness. 'One of the policemen who came to the house,' she said, 'turned out to be an authority on Romney Marsh churches. We must visit them all sometime. They were absolutely charming, the police. So helpful and considerate.'

Gerald's remains were found three days later, when the weather had calmed. The body was spotted by a bird-watcher at the foot of Fairlight Cliffs, 'incomplete' according to the police and in a state that made identification possible but not easy. Charlotte was not asked to identify it. 'No face, apparently,' she whispered, making it sound like a private scandal. 'I just had to confirm that part of his tweed jacket was his and they do the rest scientifically. It had been bashed about on the rocks, they said, which makes them think that's where he went in because the tide drift is normally easterly and he wouldn't have got there if he'd gone in where they found him last time. Which was near where we put him, of course. I had to bite my tongue to stop myself correcting them.' She tinkled again. 'I suppose the storm must have taken him out to sea and then brought him in again in a different place. No one mentioned the rug.'

There was a postmortem followed later by an inquest which concluded death through natural causes.

The postmortem showed that he was dead when he entered the water and that he had suffered a heart attack. The various contusions and lacerations were likely to have been caused by frequent violent contact with the rocky foreshore. The coroner extended his sympathy to Mrs Coombs.

Are we very bad people, Charlotte and I? Or are we merely ordinary people who have done a bad thing, which I imagine is what many bad people are? And does it matter? Yes and no. We end where nothing matters, but until we get there I suppose you would say that it does.

Thus it is that you find me here today, comfortably ensconced in a fine house in Winchelsea awaiting our friends the Marsh farmers, who are coming to dinner along with the Witneys, the retired judge and his wife, and my own special friend, Eileen, the GP. They were all so fond of Gerald. Charlotte thought it a nice idea that, two years to the day after the dinner she and Gerald gave – the last they were to do together, sadly – we should have the same company, in commemoration. Only this time Charlotte has help in the kitchen in the form of Stephanie, who lives with Millie now in our attached cottage and spends her time happily doing housework apart from the afternoons she spends with me in the shop, polishing. But she looks more to Charlotte now than to me. I feel I have lost my sister.

Charlotte and I married a year ago, also to the day. When I protested that it was less than a year since Gerald's death, quoting funeral baked meats, she said it was important not to leave these things too long. After all, we were neither of us getting any younger. We now live pretty much the life she lived with Gerald, except that I'm in the shop most days and she is free to potter about as she chooses. She likes that but she doesn't only potter. It has amused her – though she claims she does it to help me – to become an authority on sixteenth- and seventeenth-century swords. She is an astute buyer at auctions and I now sell them in the shop. The sword, meanwhile, the sword that brought us together, I have not seen since I put it down to help move the body.

'Better you don't know where it is, darling,' she said, 'in case one day you inadvertently give it away. Don't you think?'

She did not need to mention that it still has Gerald's blood on one end and my DNA and fingerprints on the other. Nor that Stuart's sword, now serving as the most expensive poker ever, is evidence of premeditation. Should I ever think of leaving her or crossing her, the authorities would no doubt believe whatever account she chose to give. After all, she is known for her devotion to Gerald. Hence our dinner party tonight.

Why me? Why did she choose me? Not, it turns

out, from desire or passion. We have not shared a bed since a few nights after Gerald's disposal when she led me to hers, permitted rather than participated in the usual thing, and afterwards said, 'There, d'you feel better now?'

Perhaps it's control, control and security, also the satisfaction of having a more or less presentable man around as a stage-prop, one without – as yet – Gerald's obvious disadvantages. And she knows how to keep me guessing. One evening, when I was poking the fire with Stuart's sword, she looked up from her newspaper and said, 'By the way, the other sword – you know the one? – did I ever tell you that it was apparently sent off once, years ago before I knew Gerald, to be examined to see if it could be Shakespeare's? Teddington or somewhere. It came back with a note saying it was a German sword made later in the seventeenth century. Too late for Shakespeare, apparently. They could tell by the steel.' She tinkled. 'I think Gerald intended to mention it to you, as you'd shown such interest, but you know how confused he was before he died. I sometimes wonder if one of the swords we buy will turn out to be Shakespeare's.'

Is that true? There's no way of knowing.

Our registry office wedding was quiet, with just Eileen and the Witneys as witnesses. 'I thought you'd like someone to tease,' Charlotte had said. 'So long as you don't make it too obvious.' In fact, I like Eileen more now. Making such an effort with her so that I could relish disliking her has had the perversely opposite effect. She makes a change from Charlotte.

Stephanie was bridesmaid, to her huge delight. She so adores Charlotte. Afterwards we lunched in a good – expensive, anyway – local fish restaurant and after that the judge was ill, which failed to sadden me. Later that afternoon as I walked Eileen to her car, she said, 'It's so nice to see Charlotte so happy again. She's had such bad luck, first with Paul and then Gerald.'

'Paul?'

'Her first husband. She's told you, surely?'

I pretended to have forgotten the name.

'He died suddenly too. Mind you, he wasn't right for her. Any more than Gerald, really. Third time lucky, I'm sure.'

I mentioned this to Charlotte that evening, as it were in passing, pretending that she had told me herself ages ago and that I'd just forgotten Paul's name. 'Eileen was quite concerned about you. She thinks you've had such bad luck, with Paul and then Gerald.'

I could see her struggling with the implication that she might have told me about Paul but forgotten. She couldn't afford to query it because she couldn't be sure what she'd said. 'Yes, poor Paul. So sad.'

'Poor you, too. How did it happen, exactly? I can't remember.'

'He fell out of a train at night. One of those old

slam-door ones, with doors you open yourself, remember? Just outside Runcorn, where we lived then.'

'How did it happen? Drink? Suicide?'

'Neither of those. Definitely not drink and no indication of suicide, no notes or history of attempts or anything like that. All a terrible mystery. No witnesses, either. He was alone in the carriage. I'd gone to the loo.'

'Perhaps he was pushed.'

'He may have thought we'd reached the station. He could be a bit absent-minded. After that I moved down here and met Gerald.'

ACKNOWLEDGEMENTS

I am very grateful to Dr Tobias Capwell, FSA, curator of Arms and Armour at the Wallace Collection, for his help and advice on swords. Any inaccuracies or inadequacies are, of course, my doing.

Alan Judd is a novelist and biographer who has previously served in the army and at the Foreign Office. Chosen as one of the original twenty Best Young British Novelists, he subsequently won the Royal Society of Literature's Winifred Holtby Award, the Heinemann Award and the Guardian Fiction Award; he was also shortlisted for the Westminster Prize. Two of his novels, *Breed of Heroes* and *Legacy*, were filmed for the BBC and a third, *The Kaiser's Last Kiss*, has been filmed as *The Exception*, starring Christopher Plummer and Lily James. Alan Judd has reviewed widely, was a comment writer for the *Daily Telegraph* and writes the motoring column for *The Oldie*.

Don't miss Alan Judd's brilliantly plotted, pulse-racing
new novel featuring Charles Thoroughgood

ACCIDENTAL AGENT

CHARLES THOROUGHGOOD #6

Brexit looms and Charles Thoroughgood, Chief of MI6, is
forbidden for political reasons from spying on the EU. But
when an EU official volunteers the EU's negotiating bottom
lines to one of his officers, Charles has to report it.

Whitehall is eager for more, but as the case develops,
Charles realises that all may not be quite what it appears.
At the same time, he finds he has a family connection with
a possible terrorist whom MI5 want checked out. In both
cases, Charles is forced to become his own agent, seeking
what he really does not want to find.

Authoritative and packed with in-depth knowledge,
Accidental Agent **is a gripping new spy thriller**
from a master of the genre.

SIMON &
SCHUSTER

Chapter One

Reflecting on it afterwards, it seemed to Charles Thoroughgood that the whole sad affair began with a wedding reception. The origins long pre-dated that, of course, germinating secretly in the characters and careers of the principal actors, but it was at that sunlit reception on the lawn of a large house in south-west London that it all began to unravel.

Or come together, depending on how you looked at it. There was, it turned out, a pattern in the carpet that Charles hadn't spotted because he wasn't looking. Even if he had looked, it would have seemed fanciful to perceive such an emerging shape. It was his failure, he had to admit afterwards; as chief of MI6 part of his job was to be alive to such possibilities but he had allowed familiarity and friendship, twin enemies of vigilance, to cloud his sight. Not to mention complacency and – harder to admit – age. The pattern was in the carpet all along but he did not see it until it was too late. Almost.

He later dated it to a precise moment at the reception, the first flickering indication that there might be a problem. The wide, red, wine-mottled face of a former colleague had grinned at him across a champagne glass and said, 'Must say, retirement's taught me what I long suspected.' He paused for Charles to respond.

Charles struggled. He remembered the man – one or two of his postings and MI6 Head Office jobs, a minor scandal in New Delhi that led to divorce, his retirement party a couple of years before. Everything except his name.

'That people have jobs to avoid work.' The red face creased in laughter, the eyes almost disappearing in folds of flesh.

Avoidance of work was something else Charles now remembered about the man. He had done his quota of that in a so-so career limited not so much by lack of ability as by lack of aspiration and a preference for the diplomatic drinks circuit over the hard graft of finding and recruiting useful agents. One of those officers who was always in or between meetings, another way of avoiding work. But the name – Jerry something? John? There were so many Johns.

'Of course, your own retirement must be coming up, isn't it? Unless MI6 chiefs can prolong themselves indefinitely, which I doubt, these days. I suppose

Gareth Horley will take over, will he? What he always wanted. Hungry Horley, we called him in Lagos. Always rushing off to the high commissioner with some titbit before telling his head of station. Usually a report that turned out to be exaggerated, putting it kindly. Mind you, with old What's-His-Face as head of station – old Thingy, you know, that madman – can't do names for the life of me these days – you couldn't blame Gareth. Jimmy Milton, that's it. Did you ever work with Jimmy? Mad as a hatter about security. Used to bury his house keys in his garden before going anywhere under alias. As if anyone claiming to live a blameless ordinary life in 123 Acacia Avenue wouldn't have the means for getting back into 123 Acacia Avenue when he got home. I remember one day when Jimmy . . .'

Charles tried to look interested without too obviously gazing across the lawn crowded with other wedding guests. He was recalling ever more about his interlocutor, but still not the name. A genial cove – a word the man would himself have used – helpful, friendly, dependable, limited, loyal. Above all, loyal, the most important quality in an intelligence officer. Lack of any other quality could be compensated for or worked around but lack of loyalty undermined everything. It was probably the most common, and therefore most underrated, quality among people in the Office. It was a given: you were part of the family, you could have rows and disagreements daily but loyalty, absolute loyalty, was taken for granted. Rightly, in almost every case. And therein lay its danger.

Interesting that the man should name Gareth Horley as his possible successor as chief. Charles had discussed his likely recommendation with no one apart from Sarah, his wife, and the cabinet secretary, to whom he answered. Gareth was director of MI6 operations, effectively Charles's deputy, promoted by him because he was everything that this nameless interlocutor was not – hard-working, with a good operational record of recruiting and running important agents, an effective bureaucrat who understood how to work Whitehall without appearing too manipulative, a charming, effective and amusing colleague. Granted, he wasn't universally popular in the Office, being seen – by his own generation in particular – as nakedly ambitious, a smiling assassin whose chief loyalty was to himself. But that was not incompatible with loyalty to the Office and to his country, and ambition was now regarded as creditable so long as it furthered the cause as well as the individual. It was different when Charles had joined decades before, when to call someone ambitious was a serious criticism. The trick then was to be ambitious without showing it; now, you were marked down on your annual assessment if you didn't display it. The change had favoured Gareth.

But no one was perfect and Charles was persuaded

that the Office would do better under Gareth than under any other in-house choice. He was also satisfied that his choice would have been the same even if he and Gareth had not been on friendly terms for years and had not, as younger officers, run operations together. Not that these days the choice of successor was any longer his; EU rules required that the post be advertised to outsiders and Whitehall might well decide that it would look more fashionably inclusive to have a woman, or someone from an ethnic minority or an out-to-grass politician to run Her Majesty's Secret Service. But his view would still carry informal clout because of his relations with the cabinet secretary and the various departmental permanent secretaries who would decide the shortlist before recommending it to the foreign secretary and prime minister. So long as he didn't make a mess of things in the meantime. Also, with Brexit the reign of EU rules was presumably coming to an end.

'One thing I wanted to ask.' The man lowered his voice and moved closer, with the exaggerated solemnity of a spaniel begging a biscuit. 'These negotiations, this Brexit stuff – I hope we're reporting on the buggers, their position papers, fallbacks and all that? Bloody well should be.'

It had become a frequent question since the Brexit referendum, easily answered. 'Off-limits as far as Whitehall is concerned. They wouldn't wear it. Spying on friends is politically more dangerous than spying on enemies. Anyway, the EU is so leaky we don't need to; it all comes out in the wash. Maybe it'll change after we've left.'

'But they're not our friends, they're trading partners who are also competitors. Anyway, countries don't have friends, they have interests. Can't remember who said that. Applies even more to intelligence services.'

Charles was relieved to spot Sarah's blue and white dress as she detached herself from the crowd and came across the lawn towards them. Luckily, he was spared the embarrassment of introductions. 'Robin,' she said, smiling and holding out her hand to the red-faced man, 'we haven't met since your retirement party. How's retirement treating you?'

'Sarah, how are you, lovely to see you. I was just saying to Charles, it's taught me what I've long suspected . . .'

Charles relaxed. Sarah, a lawyer who was not in the Office herself, was unique in having married successive chiefs and so had long experience of the kind of social chit-chat required. Also, she had a rather better memory than Charles for names and people, many of whom she knew through her late husband. She knew too that they would all have a simplified version of her and Charles's history – youthful lovers at Oxford, rivalry with the man she later married, a child sent for adoption, decades of estrangement from Charles followed by reconciliation after the disgrace and death of her husband; and Charles's role in his downfall. Knowing that this was what they would all be thinking of while talking to her, she had felt awkward and self-conscious for months after she and Charles had married but the gradual realisation that most people were more interested in themselves than others had made things easier. Now, she knew that if she didn't let the past become a problem for her, everyone else would ignore it, even if they didn't quite forget. After a few minutes she said, 'Robin, much as you two would like continue your Office gossip I'm afraid I have to grab Charles and force him to bid our farewells. He has to go back to work.'

Robin raised his eyebrows in mock, or perhaps genuine, dismay. 'What, working at weekends? Surely as chief you could get other people to do that for you?'

'Thank God you came,' Charles whispered as they walked arm in arm towards the marquee. 'I thought I was trapped there for the duration. How's it been for you?'

'I think I've got away with it so far. Just hope we can leave before I put a foot wrong. What time's this thing you're doing?'

His phone was vibrating in his pocket. He acknowledged the text. 'Okay if we leave in the next ten minutes.'

'I can't do that. I must stay a bit longer. You go off and I'll get a cab back.'

It was an Anglo-Indian wedding in the bride's parents' home in Wimbledon, a large Edwardian house with a garden the size of two tennis courts. Robin was there because he lived in the modest bungalow next door – 'The best my pension will pay for in this part of London. Not that you'll have to worry about that sort of thing, I suppose' – and Charles and Sarah because the groom, Daniel Adamson, was her godson. It was a colourful affair, the saris and costumes of the bride's family outshining and outnumbering Daniel's more soberly and uncertainly dressed relatives. Daniel, who had converted to Islam, wore a long green jacket edged with gold, his red beard trimmed and his hair cut. His bride, Akela, wore a flowing white dress, high-necked with long diaphanous sleeves and a see-through hood, the whole thing populated by what seemed to Charles to be sewn-in table-tennis balls. She smiled continuously but was generally quiet and looked nervous, unlike her parents, who were energetically gregarious and hospitable.

'But ten minutes is a bit soon,' continued Sarah. 'Can't it be longer? You must say goodbye to Deborah and everyone.'

'Everyone?'

'You know what I mean.'

Sarah was uncharacteristically brittle over anything to do with Daniel and his mother, Deborah, an old schoolfriend. She felt guilty over her self-perceived neglect of her godmotherly duties, though Daniel himself had never welcomed them.

'I'm forever on edge with Deborah and I don't really understand why,' she had admitted on their drive from Westminster to Wimbledon. 'We get on, we've never fallen out or fought over anything, there are no obvious issues. It's just that she's always so perfect in everything, always has been, which makes me feel I have to act up to her expectations – which I can't because I'm anything but perfect and it makes me nervous and I overdo it and it probably comes across to her as if I'm competing ...' She paused. '... There was space for comment there.'

'You are perfect. It goes without saying.'

'I'm not and it doesn't, which is why it needs saying.'

'She's not exactly perfect where Daniel's concerned. She's all over the place with him.'

'That's because she's hyper-defensive, which makes it worse. She can't admit she doesn't like the way he's turned out, so we all have to pretend we don't notice, and I make extra efforts to be the godmother he plainly doesn't want so that she doesn't think I disapprove. And of course my efforts fail because he never has wanted them, so I stop trying for a while and then she says something and I renew my efforts, which are obviously insincere, and he goes on as before.'

'But converting to Islam and marrying a Muslim

seems to have introduced some discipline to his life, which must surely be a good thing.'

'Let's hope. Not that it's what Deborah would have wanted for her one and only, rich though they are. Still, she's putting a brave face on it and we have to keep telling her how pleased we all are for him, which of course she doesn't believe.'

Daniel's troubled past had cost Deborah and her then husband a deal of anxiety and money. His expulsions from successive private schools, usually couched in terms of recommendations for a specialist education more suited to his needs, culminated in his absconding from the last on the eve of examinations. He was eventually picked up by the police following an outbreak of rioting in Bradford, where he had been living rough. Charges relating to public disorder were not proceeded with and there followed a decade of unfinished courses, abandoned careers, temporary unskilled jobs, expensive stays in rehabilitation units and taxpayer-funded fresh starts. Eventually, following his parents' divorce, he completed a course that qualified him as a carpenter, funded by his father as part of the divorce settlement. He found work with a small building firm in south-west London and had been a convert to Islam for a year or so before telling his parents. He changed his name to Abdul-Salaam, met and married Akela and now worked for himself.

Her family had multifarious business interests but

were mainly food wholesalers. 'I get the impression he's more religious than his in-laws,' whispered Sarah, as they approached the marquee. 'Enthusiasm of the convert, I suppose. He's stopped drinking and all that whereas they obviously have no inhibitions. But they can't be over the moon about their beloved daughter marrying a mere carpenter rather than the scion of another wealthy Indian Muslim family. And one of Jewish origin at that, albeit non-practising. Deborah's lot just look baffled, don't they?'

'His sister-in-law, Anya, seems nice. She told me Akela is a Muslim name meaning wise. It had never occurred to me. I only knew it as the name of the leader of the Cub pack.'

Anya was younger than Akela and was a trainee lawyer with a City firm. She wore a brilliant blue sari and made valiant efforts with all the groom's guests. She was the only one to mention Charles's job.

'Of course, I have to believe everything my new brother-in-law tells me,' she had said, smiling, 'but I had a moment of doubt when he told me the head of MI6 was coming to a Muslim wedding. Is that allowed?'

Charles smiled back. 'Almost compulsory now. We employ Muslims, have done for decades though no one knew it. But this is my – our – first Muslim wedding.'

'I hope you feel safe?'

'Safer here than anywhere.'

They found Daniel just inside the marquee, sipping water and patiently receiving congratulations. His beard, grown since his conversion, was neatly squared off and his previously shoulder-length hair was cut above the ears. He smiled at their approach, something he would not have done before. 'No cloaks or daggers here for you two, I'm afraid. Unless you want to disappear into the rhododendrons.'

Sarah laughed. 'Might be misconstrued.'

As they elaborated on their congratulations, Charles's mind returned to his working lunch with Michael Dunton, director general of MI5, earlier that week. He and Michael lunched monthly on sandwiches and fruit juices, alternately in each other's offices. Charles, being like red-faced Robin of a generation for whom lunchtime drinking had been a sustaining prop for the rest of the day, deferred unprotestingly to the fashion for abstinence while secretly regretting it.

'One last thing,' Michael had said. 'Sarah has a godson, I believe, who is a recent Muslim convert?' They had dealt with all their other business, the usual run of incipient turf disputes, resource allocations and personnel issues that it was in their mutual interest to resolve before they became too serious.

Charles raised his eyebrows. Any item introduced

as 'one last thing' was rarely an afterthought. 'How did you know?'

'Facebook, apparently. Not that Sarah's on it, I'm told, but the godson's mother is and Sarah features on her page. Ditto young Daniel, of course, hence some of his associates, and it's them we're interested in. A couple of them, anyway. They've been recommending certain extremist websites to him, the sort that encourage self-starters to strike a blow for Allah with knife or vehicle, that kind of thing. No indication that he's about to oblige but they're saying that converts need to prove themselves and he doesn't seem to argue with it. I only mention it because we discovered your connection with him via Sarah via his mother and all the wedding stuff and the desk officer thought you should be aware of it.'

'He's quite right. Please thank him.'

'She also asked whether Sarah would be happy to meet her and talk about Daniel in case anything looks like developing. Assuming Sarah knows him better than you do?'

'She does, yes. I'm sure she would be happy to meet her.'

'Thanks. Gareth Horley seems to be behaving himself, I'm happy to report.'

There had been an episode some months before when Gareth's exasperation with what he saw as MI5 foot-dragging over a joint terrorist case that moved regularly between Luton and Islamabad had led him to speak frankly, as he had put it. Personally abusive and bureaucratically hostile were the words used by MI5's head of operations when she complained to Michael. There were two case officers, one from each service, with the agent under MI5 control in Luton, MI6 in Islamabad. Normally, such arrangements worked seamlessly, with the agent unaware of any distinction, but in this case he had complained to his MI6 case officer that the handler he met when in Luton seemed unresponsive to his requests and had apparently failed to act on some very specific intelligence about the meeting of a potential bombing team in a flat above a bookmakers'. That was half true, in that the date of the meeting passed while MI5 and the police were still discussing whether to intervene; but in fact the meeting hadn't happened and it turned out that MI5 had another source who had said it wouldn't. The section concerned, which did not know about the joint case, had not reported the non-event to MI6, nor had news of it reached the MI5 director of operations by the time Gareth rang her to complain.

'I confess to intemperance,' Gareth had said to Charles with a smile, 'and perhaps a few expletives undeleted.'

'But what really upset them was hearing what you'd said about them to GCHQ after you'd discovered that the meeting was cancelled.'

'Okay, take your point. Though on that occasion I was complaining not so much about this incident itself as the fact that it fitted a pattern of sluggish reporting and acting.'

'Because, it seems, they have other sources reporting in the same area, not all saying the same thing. They have reason to be cautious.'

Gareth held up his hands. 'Okay, okay, I shouldn't have spoken in those terms. Point taken. Must learn to button it.'

Now, when Michael mentioned the subject again, Charles was able to take a more relaxed view. 'Glad to hear you've had no more problems. He seems to have become better behaved all round.'

'Presumably he's aware that if he wants to succeed you he needs more friends than enemies.'

This was the first of several unprompted indications that others saw Gareth as Charles's potential successor. Either Charles's mind was easily read or Gareth's record spoke for itself. 'Could you work with him?'

The response was not immediate. 'Yes.'

'With reservations?'

'Allowances rather than reservations. Allowances for temperament and manner but respect for abilities and achievements and for his reputation for making waves and getting things done.'

A reputation for making waves was not always desirable in Whitehall, despite ritual worship at the altar of change, but it was good enough for Charles. He was aware that during his own tenure he had ignored various structural and administrative issues that others thought were important. For him, they were secondary to delivering the goods and, so long as the Office delivered – in terms of intelligence produced – he preferred not to think about them. Whitehall, he suspected, thought it time for a new broom. Avoiding unpalatable tasks was one of his weaknesses, he knew.

Now, at the reception, it was refreshing to find a friendly, if somewhat solemn, Daniel, not at all the potential extremist who worried MI5. 'We had a lovely chat with Akela,' said Sarah. 'She's charming.'

'Thank you. I'm sure she will be a very good Muslim wife, thanks be to Allah, peace and blessings be upon him.'

There was no trace of irony in his round freckled face. Hard though it was for the habitually secular to take religious avowals seriously, it was a welcome change from the sullen hostility of Daniel's pre-conversion youth.

'And we chatted to Anya, her sister, too,' said Sarah. 'She seemed very nice, quite a live wire.'

Daniel nodded. 'But less devout than Akela. You've seen I've changed my name. I have a Muslim name now.' He relieved his solemnity with a smile. 'I'm surprised – grateful – you could come. I didn't think you would, given Charles's job.'

'No reason why not,' said Charles. 'None at all.'

'You know I'm a carpenter now? Really enjoying it.'

'Good religious precedent.' Charles regretted his flippancy as soon as he said it.

Daniel had to think. 'Of course, the prophet Jesus. He's only a prophet in Islam. But an important one.'

'As in Judaism.'

Daniel's smile had gone now. 'The Jews – they're another matter. Them and the Americans.' He looked down, shaking his head.

'Your new family, your in-laws, seem very friendly and sociable,' said Sarah.

'They're not as observant as Akela but that's all right, we can cope. We will lead the simple lives of good Muslims.'

Charles's phone vibrated again. 'Excuse me a moment. Work. I'm on call.' He walked back across the lawn towards the rhododendrons. The call was one he had been expecting, from Gareth Horley. 'How did it go?'

'Couldn't be better. The crown jewels.' Gareth spoke slowly and quietly, unusually for him. It emphasised both his Welsh accent and his excitement. 'We've got them, the crown jewels. One of them, anyway.'

'Where are you?'

'About to leave Heathrow. Should be at Hyde Park in about half an hour. Are you coming?'

'Yes. You'll be there first but I should make it in time.' Hyde Park was the code name for the alternative Head Office outside Reading, a fully equipped emergency headquarters maintained in case a bomb or other event rendered the normal Westminster headquarters unusable. It was fully manned for that weekend.

'I'll draft a summary for you, headlines and bullet points only. We need to discuss Whitehall circulation. Number Ten, of course, but who else? Need to know and all that but in spades this time. If it got out it could scupper the Brexit negotiations. The big story is the red line, the one we were talking about on Thursday, the one you said was—'

'Save it till I get there.

Don't miss the brilliant first novel featuring
Charles Thoroughgood

A BREED OF HEROES

CHARLES THOROUGHGOOD #1

LONGLISTED FOR THE BOOKER PRIZE

Having graduated from Royal Military Academy
Sandhurst, Charles Thoroughgood joins the Assault
Commandos and is deployed on his first tour of duty –
four months in Ireland at the height of The Troubles.

A thankless task awaits him and his men:
to patrol the tension-filled streets through weeks
of boredom punctuated only by bursts of horror.
But Charles is one of only a handful of soldiers
to have graduated university, a fact that makes
him a target for those around him, especially
his unhinged commanding officer.

As Charles struggles to adjust to army life, facing
tragedy, madness, laughter and terror, complications
in Northern Ireland begin to grow, and, quickly,
he begins to question both his place in
the army and in the real world.

SIMON &
SCHUSTER

LEGACY

CHARLES THOROUGHGOOD #2

Charles Thoroughgood, hero of Alan Judd's classic
A Breed of Heroes, has left the army to be trained
by MI6 in the arts of the Cold War.

Nothing could prepare him, however, for the
unexpected inheritance left him by his late father,
which leads him back into an old school friendship
with Viktor, a Russian diplomat living in London, and
beyond that into the murky world of Soviet espionage
at the height of the nuclear threat to the West . . .

SIMON &
SCHUSTER

UNCOMMON ENEMY

CHARLES THOROUGHGOOD #3

From a prison cell, in which he has been held
on suspicion of breaking the Official Secrets Act,
Charles Thoroughgood awaits, not only his bail,
but also the reappearance of the woman whom
all the major roads in his life have led back to.

After his years in the army and then with MI6,
Charles has begun a new chapter in his life with the
Secret Intelligence Agency, shadowing the movements
of a suspected double agent. Charles knows that he has
nothing to hide, and as he casts his mind over the course
of recent events, he begins to suspect a more sinister
motivation, both personally and politically, behind
his incarceration . . .

SIMON &
SCHUSTER

INSIDE ENEMY

CHARLES THOROUGHGOOD #4

Charles Thoroughgood is now the recently-appointed chief
of a reconstituted MI6, married to his predecessor's widow
and tasked with halting the increasingly disruptive cyber
attacks on Britain, which are threatening government
itself and all the normal transactions of daily life – not to
mention a missing nuclear missile-carrying submarine.

At the same time, another aspect of Charles's past
emerges with the murder of one of his former agents
and the escape from prison of a former colleague
turned traitor, whom Charles had helped convict.

Charles Thoroughgood ploughs a lonely furrow
in Whitehall in his belief that all these elements are
connected, a theory which dramatically gains
credibility when his wife, Sarah, is kidnapped ...

**SIMON &
SCHUSTER**

DEEP BLUE

CHARLES THOROUGHGOOD #5

During a time of political disruption and rising anti-nuclear sentiment, MI5 discovers that an extremist fringe group, Action Against Austerity, appears to have links to an established political party while planning sabotage using something or someone called Deep Blue. Banned from investigating British political parties, the head of MI5 seeks advice from Charles Thoroughgood, his opposite number in MI6.

Agreeing to help unofficially with the case, Charles must delve deep into his own past, to an unresolved Cold War case linked to his private life. Using the past as key to the present, he soon finds himself in a race against time to prevent a plot which is politically nuclear ...

**SIMON &
SCHUSTER**